Testament

TESTAMENT

Vickie Gendreau

Translated by Aimee Wall

BookThug • Toronto, 2016

FIRST ENGLISH EDITION

Published originally in French under the title:
Testament copyright © Le Quartanier, Montreal 2012.
Published with the permission of Le Quartanier.

English translation copyright © 2016 Aimee Wall

The production of this book was made possible through the generous
assistance of the Canada Council for the Arts and the Ontario Arts Council.
BookThug also acknowledges the support of the Government of Canada
through the Canada Book Fund and the Government of Ontario through
the Ontario Book Publishing Tax Credit and the Ontario Book Fund.

 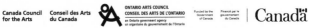

We acknowledge the financial support of the Government of Canada
through the National Translation Program for Book Publishing, an initia-
tive of the *Roadmap for Canada's Official Languages 2013-2018: Education,
Immigration, Communities,* for our translation activities.

LIBRARY AND ARCHIVES CANADA CATALOGUING IN PUBLICATION

Gendreau, Vickie, 1989–2013
[Testament. English]
        Testament / Vickie Gendreau ; translated by Aimee Wall.
—First english edition.

Issued in print and electronic formats.
paperback: ISBN 978-1-77166-252-9
html: ISBN 978-1-77166-253-6
pdf: ISBN 978-1-77166-254-3
mobi: ISBN 978-1-77166-255-0

I. Wall, Aimee, translator II. Title. III. Title: Testament. English.

PS8613.E535T4713 2016   C843'.6   C2016-904827-6 C2016-904828-4

PRINTED IN CANADA

Shelfie

A bundled eBook edition is available
with the purchase of this print book.

CLEARLY PRINT YOUR NAME ABOVE IN UPPER CASE
Instructions to claim your eBook edition:
1. Download the Shelfie app for Android or iOS
2. Write your name in UPPER CASE above
3. Use the Shelfie app to submit a photo
4. Download your eBook to any device

PAVILION A

VICKIE

Before beginning, I show you my card, you check your register. I'm the right girl, I'm the author of this book, I have access to the pavilion. In the photo, I have puffy cheeks. In the flesh, they're hollow. You're not paying attention. You concentrate on the words. I enter through the sliding door. Fireflies follow me, eight and a half by eleven fireflies. You're curious. You come to wait for the elevator with me. I tell you to take my life in your hands. The fireflies draw closer. The elevator arrives. You jump in, the fireflies too. Which floor? Third basement.

STANISLAS

She brought us all together. Me and her, me and her friends. A perfect circle, a clear-cut ring of little renown. She was careful not to name us. Like you, I'm holding the book in my hands. I'll read it at the same time as you. I'm probably going to cry too.

9

RAPHAËLLE

She wrote to us before she began her treatments, non-stop for a full day and a half. Everything that flowed through her poured into USB keys, slipped into brown envelopes to be distributed by her friend Mathieu. Poor Mathieu. It had to be difficult to know, to have known. Poor homeless fennec foxes. Poor homeless literature.

VICKIE

I have sad orange juice, the sad Virgin, sad Tia, I have no more whipped cream, I have sad tomato juice, sad green tea, a sad club sandwich, sad McNuggets pre-chewed by the blender sliding easily through the jaw, I have no more morphine, I have sad pear tea, sad brunch, totally depressed milkshake, sad pool water, sad chlorine, sad milk, sad mix, sad glass of water, sad applesauce, a champagne flute lying on its side. Sweet tears. Liquefied doughnut. Extricated ingrown hair. Underwear full of pus, sitting on the counter. It is June 6, 2012, and I'm sad. And always naked for nobody, in a big, empty bed. With this never-ending glass to finish. Other adjectives escape me. Sad attitude, sad mill, I can't sleep, I'll never sleep again.

MAXIME

A man in black approaches. He gives her a fennec fox on a leash. I see other people behind him, with more foxes. I think they'll have to use the coffin for a litter box. It's empty in any case, for now.

Centre hospitalier de l'Université de Montréal

CHUM

Week 1 – Monday

Diet: Normal, soft minced, liquid honey

Dinner

Room 5050, Bed 2

Name: Gendreau, Vickie

Please use the towelette to wash your hands before the
    meal

Berry cake

Minced meat

BBQ sauce

Diced beets

Salt

Pepper

Margarine (2)

Whole wheat toast (2)

Creamy apple beverage (3)

2% milk

Hot water

Sad tea

Decadron (1)

NIPPLE KIDMAN.COM

I would give anything to forget that I had to urinate in
one of the hospital's "guest toilets" the Monday of that
dinner. In the middle of the night. I had to hold this co-
lourful little train out of the water. It was no picnic. I'd
been fantasizing about us, happy in love in the silent sa-

vannah. As for him, he was fucking Samantha that whole time. He was telling her that her breasts are pretty. I close my eyes, I open my eyes. I'm at Mont-Tremblant. I close my eyes, I open my eyes. I'm at Mont-Laurier. I close my eyes, I open my eyes. I'm in Grand-Remous. I close my eyes, I open my eyes. I'm in Val-d'Or. I keep my eyes closed a long time. I came here to be told that my breasts are pretty. The bar is called Le 69. I'm in Rouyn. I'm one of the five pretty girls with pretty breasts promised in the lobby. The car is packed full of fennec foxes. The girls are pissed. Seven hours with a hundred foxes is a long time. No matter how cute they are. I should have put pearl necklaces on them, but I was a bit afraid that the mean girls would steal them. All strippers steal.

MAXIME

She goes out to smoke a cigarette behind the club. A man in black hands her another fox. The girls put their suitcases in the litter box, which the driver emptied and then left with. The boss gave her a double room. She hides the foxes in there, she'll go down and clean that one too. They must sell litter at the grocery store. It is May 29, 2012.

NIPPLE KIDMAN.COM

Beautiful Tatiana takes the stage. Uneventful. She leaves. Sensual Candy goes up to titillate the gentlemen. A wallet draws attention to a pile on the edge of the stage. We're in Ontario. She leaves the Ontarian stage. English girls are all the same, their names are always edible.

Sweet Camilla goes up for her two minutes. An electronic beat. It feels like twenty minutes. The Notorious B.I.G. makes an appearance in the song. Never mind. She steps down. Then Ethereal Kaya shows everyone how it's really done. The DJ has no idea what the word ethereal means. Kaya's amazing. He should have said excellent. But the other girls would be jealous. He said ethereal. She steps down. Generous Patricia takes the stage. She's fat. That's what generous means. I didn't tell the DJ a single thing about my life. He thinks I'm intelligent. Intelligence left the stage a long time ago, babe.

VICKIE

I close my eyes, I open my eyes. I'm changing my tampon on the Voyageur bus. Sketchy manoeuvre, I know. I close my eyes, I open my eyes. I'm changing my tampon at the exit of a dépanneur on Duluth. I close my eyes, I open my eyes. I see Stanislas and his new concubine walking down the other side of a grungy street in Verdun. She has more class than me, he wouldn't be ashamed to introduce her to his parents at a pseudo-fancy Apportez Votre Vin, not far from a pretty cute girl inserting a telescope into her pussy, barely hidden behind a bush. I keep my eyes closed a long time. In comparisons, I'm always the smallest one.

NIPPLE KIDMAN.COM

Before I arrive, you text me to say that Samantha was an escort for a day. Great news. Why are you telling me this? Why is it relevant? She had something to prove, no doubt. To whom? She definitely has an answer. At least I hope so, for her sake. You have to do that job for the right reasons. Otherwise kaboom, there goes your self-esteem, you can say bye to that sweet little soft ass of yours. It all goes out the window. Samantha and I are supposed to have all kinds of things to talk about because she was once an escort and I'm a stripper. This logic makes me sick. Makes me want to take a shower. We'd have Stanislas to talk about, anyway. I took a lot of showers because of that guy. In his pants, the point exclaiming for Samantha. So many client erections, so many beds. The mattress is hard, the pillow is hard, my thighs are blue. I worked hard. I did whatever I could to feed my hundred foxes.

VICKIE

I close my eyes, I open my eyes. I'm at Emergency. I close my eyes, I open my eyes. I'm still at Emergency. I close my eyes, I open my eyes. I'm on my way to the Necrology Department. I close my eyes, I open my eyes. No, it's Neurology. My breath smells like a dead fox this morning. I think again about what the oncology nurse said to me yesterday: Use condoms, my girl, you mustn't get pregnant. My breath will act as a barrier. Seeing me on my stretcher like this is not exactly a turn-on. My right breast winks at visitors through my hair. But why is your right breast always peeking out like that, anyway? Well, because I couldn't figure out my gown. It's new. There are Chinese stars on it. It's super cute with my tutu. It's pretty, but even Daniel had a hard time doing it up. Good thing the tutu is there to pull it all together. The outfit depends on it. Yes, I'm wearing a tutu in my hospital room. I'm in bed, in front of the empty chairs for visitors. The two empty chairs are pushed up against the wall. At any moment now, one of the comedians from Les Appendices, Dominic Montplaisir, and his girlfriend could show up to tell me that they're going to name their baby Amandine Montplaisir. Amender son plaisir, enhance your pleasure, I think that's hot, it's poetic. At any moment now, Jim Jarmusch could come in to sing me "I Put a Spell on You" with his cigarette voice. At any moment now, the poet Andrés Morales could show up in boxer shorts with whiskey and offer me a Marlboro. I'm craving nicotine. I'm craving peace. I will always be craving something in order to be happy. Time, ultimately. Right now, the chairs are empty, the possibilities are infinite, all the bums that could potentially fill these seats. Divine could come sing me "Female Trouble," the giant rapist lobster could dance on the other chair. It would disturb Madame Tardif less if Divine whispered. Madame Tardif is the woman who shares my room, she's had a big operation on the vertebrae in her neck. Her lymphatic fluid gives her pain down to her legs. I'm a bit jealous. I'd like to be operable, too. She's nice, she puts up with all my visitors. Stanislas could come watch me sleep, stroke my hair. Stanislas will always be the man of my life, I'm just not the woman of his. I'll explain that later. Later in this little book, later in my little life. I thought that I was going to write this book and then never speak of the subject, the boy, ever again. Everything is imperative in my life now. This is probably the last heartache I'll ever have. The last times hurt. Life is vulgar. I would like to at least be able to chill out for a few weeks in the library with Genet and Guyotat. I won't bore you with that too much. My stories never work. That's why I like poetry, it's always infinite. I'm suspicious of people who end their poems with a period.

NIPPLE KIDMAN.COM

I can't stop thinking about it. About your cock between Samantha's legs while I'm here all saccharine in my .doc, unable to stop thinking about you. Imagining you kissing me. This new reality, this membrane frozen over. During this time, you'd meet her son. You played Wii with her son. You must love her, some part of you. You would never have met my son. If I'd had one. I aborted all three of them. That photo album doesn't exist. No beautiful family portraits. What if I sent you some dirty pictures. She stole my lover. You look at the naked photos of me together in her big, white bed in Verdun. I'm so stupid. Big, hairy and stupid. I should have known. But I thought you would ask yourself the minimum number of questions. Two psychologist parents. Apparently not. I was wrong. It's like those girls who think they're in love because they didn't use a condom with the guy. You justify your irresponsibility and I write in 125%.

VICKIE

The doctors always make me repeat it, it's June 6, 2012, I'm an obedient parrot, it's my father's birthday. The doctors tell me that I have a "cloud" tumour in my brain stem. The doctors crash my party. The sequins cloud over. Later, I thought of my father as I pulled off my electrodes before the millionth MRI. My mother accumulates old visitor badges and cards for my appointments in her huge purse. Isabelle bought a cloth bag with multicoloured butterflies. Francis decorated my room with leftovers from Dollarama. Balloons that say "Happy Birthday" when you've just learned of your imminent death are kind of in bad taste. My friends are nice at heart, that's the important part. They're funny, they say that the doctors are always asking me the date when they come to my room because they're too spaced out to remember it themselves. For the time, it's the man in 5048. For the lunch menu, it's the lady in 5049. For the date, it's the girl in 5050. Isabelle called the hospital's film library the other afternoon to ask if they had the latest Xavier Dolan. No, madame, this is just for the serious things of life, no butter, no popcorn, no jujubes, sorry. June sixth two thousand twelve. I could write it out for you on a piece of paper, but my hand's so paralyzed that I write like a three-year-old now, according to Sébastien anyway. There are so many common names to retain, but I'm telling you, I retain nothing. I bring you back into my daily life, my private life. You must have a friend named Julien. I would like for you to talk to me about your friend Julien. I remember. My aunt Julienne had given me temporary tattoos of butterflies for Christmas when I was fourteen. She'd surprised me staring at a butterfly hovering around a sunflower in her yard.

I was staring at the butterfly the way Mathieu stares at the bread sometimes when he watches me eat. A few months later, this present. Aunts are all so terribly literal and uniformly lacking in originality. But sometimes an aunt is like a sister, and I know there must be some kind of cool foremothers out there somewhere.

NIPPLE KIDMAN.COM

Sexy Kimora moves toward the steps. Fuck, I have the same dress as her for my slow one. I'm going to have to put something else on. Four steps, the stage. I can't stop staring at her. The dress looks better on me, I have more of an ass. Everyone in the room wants to marry her, me most of all. No, I'll never get married. It was Stanislas or nobody. For real, though, I would be happy that they found each other, he and Samantha. Happy for them for real. I'm ridiculously altruistic, which is not far from what love is, of course. I would be jealous, for sure, but there are things that pass us by. Love is one of them, that I know. The thing is that I know him, Stanislas, and he doesn't give a shit. He just wants to get his dick wet. Being nice, meeting her son, it's a soft approach with a hard result. There isn't a shower on earth big enough to contain all my disgust. Makes me want to write at 200%. I vomit a hairball, the size of the head of a little boy with endlessly long hair like Rapunzel's. That's important in a ball. In the fetal position, obviously. Poor little boy.

MAXIME

A little boy dressed in black approaches, hands her the

leash of a fennec fox. There's an army of toddlers behind him. She cannot refuse refuge to a being as magical and badass as the fox. Even if she has to move to accommodate everyone.

Centre hospitalier de l'Université de Montréal
CHUM
Week 6 – Thursday
Diet: Normal, soft minced
Dinner
Room 5050-02
Name: Gendreau, Vickie
Please use the towelette to wash your hands before
  the meal
Beef and scallop soup
Ice cream à la jeune fille
Salt
Pepper
Ground poultry
Poultry gravy (Separate, 4)
Diced mixed vegetables
Potato puree
Margarine (2)
Whole wheat toast (2)

2% milk
Hot water
Tea bag
Creamy apple beverage (3)
Decadron (1/2)

PAVILION B

VICKIE

At night, I smoke cigarettes outside of Pavilion B. The pavilions are connected to the main building. My room is in A. It's cold out, I'm wearing a bathrobe. You don't smoke, but you keep me company. I'm the one who's going to die, not you, not yet. The firefly that wouldn't leave you alone flies off and another takes its place, as if to protect you from second-hand smoke.

EYE'S WIDE TWAT.DOC

I remember the kids who left, the lit streetlights. I remember mostly why I left. Caprice (the girl, not the word) was telling some story. It's what girls do, whine and tell stories. I have a vagina and what really gets on my nerves is when people use the full name of someone we all know, just to make themselves seem important. Seriously. I get it, Samson, when you give me a hard time for naming all the people in my stories even if the reader doesn't know them. It's annoying. Both my ex and my best friend are named Mathieu. I also get it that you, Caprice, want to seem well-connected. But calm down. It's just a journalist. When you start a sentence with "my friend So-and-so," I don't believe you. Nobody does. You fall in love with a guy after sleeping with him once. Without fail. You have a pretty loose idea of friendship. I don't even want to imagine what would have happened if you'd slept with your famous journalist. What were you going to do? Add a few words, a little paragraph on the length and thickness of his cock? See what I mean? And you still wouldn't have started your story. I pull out my demagnetized metro pass. There's a lineup. In front of me, a guy and a girl, two cell phones.

— I stretched out in the park and read my book, says the guy in front of me into his phone.

— There was a bird caught in the window, says the girl in front of me into her phone. I was in the little shop at the corner of Pap and Laurier. The one where I bought my hat. You like my hat? It's funny, right?

— Jean Genet. *Les nègres*. Funny thing to read in a big, sunny park.

— I was thinking that a baby bird might have touched it, my hat. That's sort of why I bought it.

— Would've been nice to have some chocolate to go with my pineapple. Yeah, I have some left in a Tupperware. I didn't finish the book. I didn't get anything done today.

— I started singing "La Vie en rose" to the other one,

the girl who was shouting, short hair and big eyes. It was super cute with my hat.

— Nigga, please.

— Like a French Liza Minnelli.

— One ticket, please.

— Oh, some guy in front of me. But I'm going to get two tickets, I'll probably come back tonight.

The guy realizes: the girl is looking at him intensely. Bonjour, tension.

MAXIME

The guy at the wicket holds out a key to Vickie, winking. He whispers: the bike rack, in front of the station. She thought she'd seen something squirming and sparkling through the filthy window, like in a video game, a soft porn film from the seventies, a race in slow motion – fifteen wriggling fennec foxes. She's going to need a bigger bag.

EYE'S WIDE TWAT.DOC

Everyone's talking on the phone. Mine is dead and nobody calls me anyway. They didn't even call me to let me know that Max had killed himself. I found out by email. A friend is dead and people can't stop laughing. On Facebook, everybody goes on with their lives and I do too. I go on, doing nothing, contemplating my news feed. It reminds me of when my grandmother was in the hospital. I'd found out through email. Life is fragile and it just goes on. Raphaëlle was angry at Caprice.

"She organized the picnic in memory of Max like you'd organize any old get-together. She just wants to drink." She was right. I gave one of my beers to Caprice. The day of the email, I was mixing orangeade into my vodka. I'd forgotten to buy juice. The neighbour's kids were making a ton of noise. It was crazy up there, up above my head and inside it, too. The kids go to bed late. I could still go to the store to buy juice. To Videotron to return the movies I didn't have the time to watch. I'm totally vegetative right now. This is my first drink, I'm hoping the vodka will give me energy to go for a walk. That's what normal people do, go for walks. After dinner, to digest, to think. With the kids, to take them to McDonald's for a surprise. To the park or the shoe store, everywhere, anywhere for a surprise. My cousin Anabel, when she was the same age as the kids upstairs, had more shoes than my Barbies. Her own personal Panda Shoes, they didn't even all fit in her closet. I remember the alluring chaos of the hallway. I would show up when I hadn't been invited. At Christmas, it was always well organized. In my mind, there are two kids, the same age, the kids upstairs, I mean. I'd like to go for a walk. Max is dead. He committed suicide. They're all committing suicide all the time. We lead difficult lives, my friends and I. He wasn't a close friend. He committed suicide either way. In my mind, the kids upstairs are diabolical. They're a part of my circle. Two little girls, constantly jumping and shouting. Suicidal parents. Eloquent, future cheerleaders, slightly intelligent bimbos, just smart enough, chatty extroverts, drama queens. Right now, they're just two little idiots jumping and shouting. I wonder what's actually happening up there. What real life is like for these people. I stayed on Facebook all day. I watched the news feed scroll. I won't recount what people were saying. I'm not here on this earth today to report the facts. Max threw himself off a viaduct. The day before, he'd asked if I had a number for MDMA. I didn't. Maybe I should have had one, and I should've more than this old bottle of orangeade to mix with my vodka. You can't take Smirnoff straight.

Can't take the death of a friend straight, either. I don't even have a full bottle. Samson says that what I'm drinking is called student sangria. I find that funny, ironic, but I don't dare laugh.

I don't dare read much, either. I'm pretty much useless. But whatever.

Eat me on a bagel. I'm a smoked student.

Never go back to school, just be ready for it.

MAXIME

I started by swinging a fox off the viaduct, then a second one, then a third. Two hundred, then three hundred. She caught them all in her big bag. A bottomless catch-all. I jumped, but there was no room left inside. Sorry.

POULIN ROUGE.DOC

There are no mistakes on the signs carried by the waves of student protesters. There's no little pool of red light to indicate where to find Stanislas and his new concubine in the crowd. There's no little group of frustrated femi-

27

nists like I imagined, severe women who sneer and judge. Why is nobody sneering and judging? I should have worn a skirt, I could have sneered. It would have been the same. I don't judge. I'll never be important enough to judge. I would so like to be severe and frigid. I'd like to be stupid and ugly too. I'd like to not reduce the world down to two adjectives. I don't even want to imagine what mine would be. They wouldn't be flattering. Maybe I am severe and frigid in the end. We are marching against adversity. We are all dressed up in red in our own ways. My eyes are always full of red. They were brown a few weeks ago. Brown like what you leave in the toilet. All the same, it's a more encouraging colour than red. I cried more tears than were in my body. Because of this guy. We are so many things. I am touching and full. But vain. Like this crowd: vain. In my life: vain. I don't think I'm pretty anymore. I'm still crying over my failed creamed corn, I cry over everything all the time. I cry with my eyes, my nose, my mouth. I keep repeating the possessive adjective because I often feel like I'm a stranger to my own face. I put my eyes back into my own face because these eyes belong to me, so as to not forget that, to not cease to exist, to be able to see. Reality bores me. It depresses me. I'd like to be called Samantha. I'm angry at my mother. Why not Samantha? She doesn't respond. I'm depressing her. She looks for me in the newspaper but doesn't find me. Tomorrow, I'll say: Look, Maman, I'm somewhere in that crowd. I hope the headline isn't too nasty. Somewhere in that crowd. There is no area code to contain my sadness. I could go work far away from here, far from the guy, but I'd always be this melancholy. The whole universe is black nihilism. I see hippies with big, plastic trumpets in the crowd. They're making noise. But then, everyone's making noise. Nobody's listening. You can't listen to photos, you can just put them in the newspaper with nasty headlines. I'll take a photo with my phone. Oh right, I don't have one anymore. I couldn't give my mother's phone number to the police if I got arrested. I have to stay calm. Far from the headlines. I'd like to be a little bad, though. The hippies go on and on with their noise. I stretch out my arm, it's infinitely long, it's a ribbon. I grab hold of a trumpet and put it to my lips. I've got something to say too.

In the crowd, there's no group of strippers with their signs: MY PUSSY IS AGAINST THE HIKE. There are no journalists with feathers in their asses. There's nobody sleeping, no serenity, not a drop of rosé. In the crowd, there are no cherry trees. There's no bathroom. There's no lineup at the library. There's no lineup at the dépanneur.

I close my eyes, I open them. I'm at the dépanneur, buying black cherry juice.

MAXIME

Noise from inside the beer fridge, little cries. Fennec foxes, assorted cases of foxes, zero percent foxes. She takes a case of a dozen iced tea–flavoured foxes.

POULIN ROUGE.DOC

The hippie whose trumpet I snatched leaves in a taxi to find it. My driver, the dancers' driver, tells me that if I'm poetic, then he's a poem. I want to cry. I cry. I do what I like. I'm a princess. Trash royalty, but a princess all the same.

— Where to, mademoiselle?

— Not school.

VICKIE

There will always be a collection agency to wake me up in the morning. There will always be a pot of something rotten in my fridge. There will always be someone to hate me. Someone to make a fool of me on the telephone at three in the morning. Someone to treat me like a slut in front of my family. Someone to steal my drink, someone to steal my purse.

POULIN ROUGE.DOC

Exit Moody Boulevard North.

Pass by La Plaine, Jane.

Arrive at a strip club in a redneck's red pickup: check.

Feel sad: check.

Write original erotic stories for Stanislas: check.

Client who smells of patchouli: came.

Lip-synch the words of "Sexy Sushi" on stage: check.

Do a number to "Raise Your Weapon" and lift a leg
   during the chorus: check.

Client who drives a huge Benz: came.

Drink a Nitrous Yellow Monster in two gulps: check.

Eat an endive salad in three bites: check.

Throw out the leftover sesame shrimp from the
   restaurant: check.

Go to a funeral in a babydoll: check.

Raphaëlle loaned me the babydoll. Stanislas Merdier, Anne Archet and 8 others have tweets for you. But that's all they have for you. I met a client who had the Enlarge Your Penis machine. One of my condoms met his penis, his money met my wallet, and later on that day my face met the closed door of the fish market. They have tweets for you. That's all they'll ever have for you. Consider yourself lucky, fille. Respond with something witty. Say yes constantly without knowing the question. Say yes and skip. It's exhausting, singing while working this hard. You're allowed a rest, girl, take a break. Eat your granola, drink your coffee. Listen to your loud, annoying music, get annoyed, but don't forget you have to look after the animals. The speakers are blasting, the foxes dance. It's annoying. Something important is happening. A black fly is chilling not far from a fox. They aren't like cats, the foxes, they don't hunt insects. They dance. Felix Cartal provides the beat. The fox extends a paw, the insect too. I have Felix in my headphones. The black fly is suddenly in Raphaëlle's hair. I thought we were somewhere else and that it was a brooch. I'm always surprised, always lost. I'm usually always at the hospital. But Raphaëlle took me out today. Nice surprise. It's Max's funeral today. She brought a pile of beautiful black clothes. I don't even remember anymore if I asked, if I was polite. I don't remember anything. It's fun, missing pieces like that. Everyone misses pieces. I remember everything, absolutely everything. Remembered. Verb tenses hurt. Especially when it's about you, and it's you who's writing them. I chose the babydoll from the pile of black clothes. I went to the funeral with that on my back. Yeah, I'm that kind of girl. A bit slutty. You love to hate me.

I'm at Kingdom, corner of Saint-Laurent and
  Sainte-Cath.
Mindy and Trevor examine my body with their
  sticky hands.
Nikky is beautiful.
More beautiful than me.
More fluid than me.
I fall down everywhere.
I close my eyes, I open my eyes.
I'm in New York.
In front of the cage of fennec foxes at the
  Brooklyn Zoo.
I got special permission to pet them.
I close my eyes, I open my eyes.
I see Austria, I meet Ulrich Seidl.
He tells me about his next film.
I close my eyes, I open my eyes.
I'm at a noise show with the dudes from
  Granular Synthesis.
I close my eyes.
I keep them closed a long time.
I will do none of these things.
On Sunday, I'll go to Beautys with my friends, drink
  a Cookies & Creme milkshake.
That, I'll do.
Eyes open, wide.

To Stanislas, I bequeath:
these two texts,
a piano-playing cat
and two hundred fennec foxes.

STANISLAS

I come across as a dirty dog. She says she took a lot of showers because of me. But I knew just how to earn her love until the end. A city needs a lot of one-way streets to make us appreciate the ones that run both ways. Love Boulevard. That girl was way too intense. Too much passion in one girl. I met her in that bookstore. I'm standing in front of the door, I can't go in, it's closed. Somewhere in the world, it's raining.

STARGIRL SATAN.DOC

I will not be that stupid girl. I could be all the others, just not that one. I will not change your name in my book in the hopes that one day you'll talk to me again. I'll go on being the devil. The devil who screws with the heads of all those stupid little girls, one after another. I'll sow my seed. Even if there's no earth, no soil, even if it's just a warp zone of fallow land. You were there, next to me in the bookstore, right there. It was for a book launch. You were right there, a bicep curl away. And my lips. Oh, my lips. I wash the glasses to distract myself. I hide in the little vestibule to wash the dishes and I cry. You'd think I want to wash the glasses to be nice, but really it's to cry, to bawl my eyes out even. The booksellers think I'm nice, but really I'm just crying. Crying in the back room. Two faucets just above my nose. At least I'm safe here, nobody can disturb me or worry about me. My head in the sand, and in the dishes. The little glasses sparkle. I wonder if I could fill an icecube tray with the weepy wailing spilling from my face. I've got a degree in Managing Shit but no room left in my backpack. Enough is enough. My red bag is too red. My hair is too curly. And there are too many people here. My hair was curly like this when we met.

STANISLAS

I met Vickie at Port de tête. I was going out with Alexie at the time. I'd never heard her name before. She said I seemed horribly pretentious. I plugged their Gala for the Academy of Literary Life at the Turn of the 21st Century. I think I was nice. She thought I was pretentious. I was maybe not ready to meet her. She was wearing the same sequined hat when I met her again later on. She remembers everything, absolutely everything, that girl.

STARGIRL SATAN.DOC

The man of my dreams, right there, for a while now. I'm avoiding him, I stand far away. He's been talking about his pigeon infestation for a while, about his life without me, entirely without me. I'd almost forgotten that I'm the devil. The devil is not the type to cry. That's something, at least. I'm at least that much human. I stay in the little vestibule for a few minutes. I watch the door, I'm afraid he might show up. I'll pour what's left of my face into the sink again. I check that I'm safe, then plop, the whole sink is filled in one shot. I go out onto the terrace. Smoke alone. Far from other faces. If I don't have a face, nobody does. A proverb. More in love with him than he is with me. Another proverb. My leather ankle boots are damp. A big hole in the right foot. Humidity doesn't know gravity. My pocket vibrates. I'd almost forgotten that there's a cell phone in my life, that you can reach me when I put some minutes on it. Or when I can find it in the mess of my bedroom. Completely forgotten that I was sending vibrations to my friends' pockets a little while ago. My friends are here. I have to find them. They're inside. I go in. I look for capes. I find their trench coats. Where's Stanislas? Look into the little bus mirror perched between the books. Proust, Proust, Nietzsche and me, not a writer. I'm a long way from literature. Between the two rows. Trying to memorize the titles of films people suggest to me. More wine. More melancholy. More wine. Didn't dare touch it before, but my friends are here now. Kleenex, little white capes that you fish from coloured boxes. I'm coloured. My sleeve is a tissue. For now. We go back out onto the terrace because I need to smoke. Being sad stresses me out. Fuck, yes. You're here. You ask how I'm doing. I find that question ridiculous. I don't answer. I'm going to implode. I tell you that my birthday's on Saturday.

STANISLAS

I reread every email she sent me, I reread her last one. It's been months, years, a long time. I stare at the package that Mathieu sent me, distracted. I put it on my desk. I'm a bit freaked out. She was crazy about me. Now, she's dead. I was at her funeral. She wasn't there. Her body was in the black box. She left super fast without saying bye to anyone. That morning, instead of putting on a sparkly dress, the shirt I gave her and her eternal black leggings, her fuzzy skirt with that awful sweater covered in horses... instead of all that, that morning she put on a black box. Finito.

STARGIRL SATAN.DOC

I hide in the shadows and dig in my purse. I find something to smoke. At least I can smoke. The guy doesn't give a shit about me, but at least I can smoke something, something that belongs to me, just to me, this cigarette, metaphor, match, melancholy, gasoline. Smoke myself. And smoke these lousy memories. But never see the end of it. An unlimited package. Maybe we have to lose ourselves in the simple things. Maybe that's the only place we can properly lose ourselves. My friends are leaving. Laure is here to remind me that the last time we saw each other I was so drunk and sad that I fell down. I made myself so beautiful. I'd like to talk to Laure about my love problems. She's a girl, she'll get it. I want to spew my love problems all over other people, but I have nothing to wipe them up with afterward. I wasn't made for all this. I found a blue-flowered jacket in my boxes this afternoon. I could wear that to my birthday. Fuck my birthday. Fuck the entire month of April. I feel like I'm going to end up crying on Saturday. Because I thought, yes. We'd made plans, yes. So many plans. My birthday. My thoughts repeating. I leave the bookstore so that nobody will see me crying. Flowers for nobody. I'll weave a necklace of flowers and offer everything that flows out of me. To whom? To nobody. Vickie Who? Vickie Nobody. I'm everyone and nobody at the same time. Félix seems disgusted by the world around him. I get it. The stairs ahead. I pass a girl. She asks me if I'm okay. I explode or implode, I don't know anymore. I think that I haven't completely given up, I was sane up until then. Why? I don't know. I'm the devil, that I know. Two other girls come outside. One's named Ariane, she's the girl who looks like Pippi Longstocking from behind. She tells me she's waiting for Laure and Stanislas. To go to a show. She asks me how I'm doing. I choose to hear only every second word. Because it seems more fun to imagine than to know. We talk, we talk. He comes out. You come out. The girls leave. I feel like I'm going to cry. I want it to happen more quickly. You're wearing a button-down shirt. She looks like she smells good. You smell so good. I would kiss you all night. I would spend my whole life showering you with compliments. I said none of this. No. I thought about rabbits, about Radio Radio, Ryan Gosling in a jacuzzi. Nobody lets their kitten out on Mont-Royal at night. Or during the day. The kitten definitely washes the dishes all day long in the back room.

STANISLAS

I made love to a bunch of other girls and I'm not stingy with my lust. I'm selective. It doesn't bother me to be a little chaste. It's just summer, it's hot out, that's all, it's understandable. What I do with my body is nobody's business. I think it's a little because of this that she wanted us to stop talking. She pretty much knew what was up and it worried her that she didn't know everything. I wouldn't have answered anyway. All or nothing with that girl. I went to Italy. She knew how to say one word in Italian. Uccello. It means bird. It's not really useful in any practical sense. You can point at the birds and say what they are. The language level of a seven-year-old kid. At most. Note that a bird doesn't keep still, it could be hard to know what she was pointing at if she didn't specify. The kind of girl who could point to a particular cloud, a dense little one over the garden let's say, and tell you about it for hours. Long descriptions worthy of great novels or strung-together foolishness worthy of little rags. All-terrain girl. She could have pointed out the cloud, the plane or a patch of the stratosphere, but she always focused her energy on the bird. The bird is important.

STARGIRL SATAN.DOC

Pierre is definitely at Bar Inc. I could definitely fuck Pierre. It's not important who he is. I could fuck the whole world. Some would even pay. But I won't do it. No. I'm only capable of fucking a stranger when I'm drunk. But in any case, I always end up talking about Stanislas. About you. We don't fuck. I console myself. And the next day, I regret it. And the day after that, I find the freezer cozy. I forget. Everything except the guy I should forget. You sit next to me. My face goes crazy. My eyelid twitching incessantly. A brown car passes by the bookstore. Something enters me and refuses to leave. You're right there. I don't understand anything anymore. I say things. I respond. Sentences gush out. Félix crosses the road, I see him through my tears. I'm crying. Oh. I'm the devil. But the devil who writes well. But the devil who no longer writes. So write. Go elsewhere. You leave. Yes. You leave. I turn around and you've disappeared. It's fine, it's better. It's good like this. It's stupid. I'm stupid. I cried. I can't stop myself anymore. Mathieu crosses the road. Everyone crosses. Everyone sees me, but I see nothing. I'm boring, wet and sad. People cross and the people who cross like what I write even if I don't write anymore. I already wrote enough for a few more days. I can do very little with my evening now, I can just cry while listening to sad music. My hairspray smells like lilies of the valley. My little foot powder, too. The humidity reminds me of it. I met a girl at a rave who was named Lily. She had only one arm. We felt like butterflies. Lily had just one wing, but she was still a butterfly. To go into my cocoon. To forget the guy. So I can go out and never end up drunk because I'm too sad. Too sad to forget. I'm going around in circles. I remember everything. Everything. Not him.

Me, yes. Not you. Not a big deal. So many friends. God, I just talk their ears off. I don't give a shit. Ears grow back. Hair too. So burn it. An idea. So that people will go away. The staircase is my staircase. My body is my body.

STANISLAS

When I watch the Mr. Peabody video, the nice baby owl taking his bath, I think about her. The moment someone says something about fennec foxes, I see her face. She would have wanted it this way. Uccello, fennec. Vickie. Three little periods. I always hated exclamation points. She said she'd stopped writing. It's not true. I felt the brown envelope that Mathieu sent me. I'm pretty sure there's a USB key in there. Today, Vickie is wearing a USB key and a brown envelope, it's cold out, it's winter. She's naked underneath. Always naked, that girl.

STARGIRL SATAN.DOC

A friend comes to see me. He takes me in his arms without saying a word. I ask him why. He tells me that I look like I'm about to explode. It's the end of the night with the dubstep. I start crying uncontrollably. Fireworks that can't quite get it up. The driver calls. He's there. I cross the road. I climb in. Finally. Why finally? Why the big deal? I got all dressed up for nobody, for nobody who wants me, in any case. I love a man who doesn't love me back, not as I am, in any case. You don't want to talk to me anymore, but you like nudging me. I'm not your guy friend, dude. Come on. I'm a breakable little girl. And I was hot all over just because of your little nudge. All this desire and all this love, yes it's definitely love, all of it wasted. On a boy I still dream about every day. I'll curl up naked in my pillows and tomorrow, my client will call me to have dinner. He'll tell me that I'm beautiful, that the boy is stupid for not wanting me, because I'm a fucking catch and all that. The dancers' driver told me, to "console" me, that all boys are rapists at heart. But not all of them, monsieur. I don't know your boys, but I know this one with the elbow from just now, and he is absolutely extraordinary. This is why it's so difficult.

STANISLAS

I can't go back to the bookstore to cry in the same spot she did. I can't cry without the bookstore. The bookstore is closed. There are no more students. Outside, it's the apocalypse. The end of the world in winter. I remember Vickie had told me about a Mayan symbol that represented a waking death. She wanted to tattoo it on the back of her neck. I didn't check to see if she'd done it. I didn't lift her skull from its cozy little cushion. Her coffin didn't seem like an adequate clothing choice. The little cushion offended me with its cozy pout. She never published a book. I wonder if Mathieu will take it on. I'm sure she hears me, that she's awake. I spoke to the prettiest of the plants when I whispered to her that I did like her a lot anyway.

I insert the USB key into its slot finally. I inspected it thoroughly beforehand. I wore a condom to sleep with her. I'm vigilant. I feel a little sick. In the Finder window, I can see that the key is named Cuntjuice. I don't even remember the taste anymore. Just what it looked like. A mole in the centre, at the top, so small it could have been mistaken for a hair. I remember. She told me that her stepfather had taken the mole on her hand to be a bit of chocolate. He couldn't know. I wonder what he would think of me. He's Italian. Italians like me. I know how to say more than a single word.

FUCK MEOW HARDER.DOC

You said: I find it so cute, a girl writing. It's like a cat that plays the piano. You said it was a joke, I said it wasn't funny. I meow and I play the piano. I would go out for tea with you, but there's a man coming to "tune my piano." It's just that I only write out of melancholy and fury, and that's not cute. I'm not cute when I write. I cry, I get all snotty, it gushes out. Not cute. Not meow. But from now on, yes. I will wear beautiful clothes to write in. I'll curl my hair, I'll wax my brows, my bikini line, too. I'll put on girly music and bounce around. I'll be like a feather duster on ecstasy. Meow. I'll wear my Festival of Love badge over my heart. My chest will taste like strawberries, or rhubarb. The unanticipated jugular pulsates. A fancy adjective and then a verb, the significance of which I ignore. I'm cute, don't forget. The soldiers will have foam swords. And me, I'll be pretty. I'll tell you that this was all just a dream. Hummingbird eyelids. I'll let you touch my politics with your big, hairy, man hands. The little nationalist deluge, with girl with an informed look. The activist look works well for other young women. Piano.

STANISLAS

She's not always nice. Not always nice forever. This will never end. I explained to her that it was a joke. I told her she was twisting my words. She responded with something vague. I understood that I'd made her want to take a shower and that she'd done so. There must still be a trace of that shampoo in her hair.

FUCK MEOW HARDER.DOC

I'm positive that this has already happened to you too. You with your vagina, or you who can imagine having one. Nobody will admit it. It's too personal. It involves just you, the fridge, and the night. I'm not ashamed. Bold as brass, or stainless steel. The night is totally clear. I'm that kind of bird. Meow, piano. You get up to drink juice from the carton. Why bother with a glass, nobody's watching. Drinking while thinking, it's always messy. Beatrice Lemonade. It costs like two dollars. It's not worth any flourish, no crystal needed. You're worth it, without question, but why bother, nobody's watching. So you take a couple swigs from the carton. In a nightdress. In what looks like a sweater for the daytime but has become a nightdress. Baggy clothes. Mathieu says you're pretty when you wear baggy things. Meow, piano. The lemonade spills, your chin glistens, the liquid runs down your skin. On your belly, it meets the dress: it's as if your belly button peed. It continues to run, to flow down. It stops short at the top of your mound. You're still standing, your back arched. Professional requirement. That's how we look cute in high heels, when we drink juice from the carton on our way to piss in the middle of the night. Meow, piano. I write these lines with an arched back.

STANISLAS

That has never happened to me. I'll nod along, but that has never happened to me. I sleep naked. Sometimes in boxers. I don't even want to imagine what she would have done with my boxers if I'd left her a pair, as a souvenir. I just emptied the contents of the envelope onto the kitchen counter. My shirt fell out with a disgusting sound, like a handful of boiled spinach onto a porcelain plate. What did you do to this pretty shirt, poor girl? I think again of the name of the USB key and I'm a little frightened. Maybe I should wear gloves.

FUCK MEOW HARDER.DOC

Mathieu says that if I spend three days on the couch with my current set-up, I'm going to look like the little girl in *The Grudge*. That's funny. Arch your back, little girl. Type your tax forms with an arched back. Type your angry little texts, your back arched. Lose your mind, back arched. Meow, piano. I didn't wipe up the spilled lemonade. I'll get up. Marriage material. I'll cook too, while I'm at it. I'm making a pot of chili. I need to find smoked eel for tomorrow. I need a bargaining chip. I'm inviting myself to dinner at his place tomorrow, it's decided. He'll never invite me himself. A smoked eel in exchange for sex. A barter. I could wait for him in the living room while he puts on music, unwrap the eel, lay my clothes on the couch, get into a bridge pose and put the eel around my pelvis, as if it was a belt. Table woman. Maybe I'm crazy but it'd make me laugh. He might also laugh. He's a Louperivois, he was born in Rivière-du-Loup and then moved to Montréal. He might get it. The fish shop is closed. My pussy is sad. The taxi driver tells me that there's another. Let's go. Meow, piano.

STANISLAS
Fuck. Why don't I love you? Seriously. You're perfect. Is that what you want me to say? You're kind of the one who decides. Making macramé out of my vocal cords. Weave, little idiot. Keep weaving. Make me say everything you hope to hear. Weave more, harder. So that I fuck meow harder. Not you, another, someone else. It's summer, I'm hot.

FUCK MEOW HARDER.DOC
Smoked eel takes less time to cook, he started to explain to me earlier. It'll be basic eel at this point. Then I thought I could hang it from the overhead light in the living room and just smoke like a chimney, as usual, and that would be that. Take your time, oven, I have lots to say with my body to your owner. I could dance for him. That would help me create a distance. I could take a photo with my computer. Yes. To ask him to dinner. Like a funky invitation. I could write the word ROCK on a Post-it, stick it on my forehead and crouch down on the packaging of the eel, hold it under my face. I'll be the proverbial anguille sous roche, the something fishy go-

ing down. It's dark in the second fish shop. Nobody sells fish in the dark. They sell fish at the IGA, the driver tells me. I'd catch the dumb eel myself if I had the time. We just passed by a fountain. If I were an eel, I'd be there. Go for the IGA. Meow, piano.

STANISLAS

It's not true. I don't believe you. You wouldn't have taken a forty-dollar taxi to zigzag from one fish shop to another. It would have been so merciful, to love you. I could have eaten smoked eel every night. I would have been your pimp. I would have sent you everywhere, across all of Québec, so that you could bring back everything I want to eat. A boy king. Go, young queen, go to Abitibi, it's hunting season. Bring me fresh meat, make me a stew. Pots clanging. Ding. It's ready.

FUCK MEOW HARDER.DOC

The driver tells me that he'd get me to dance. That I'm so pretty, so nice. If only he knew how I'm never enough, how I'll never be enough. I tell him that my client said I should call myself Snow White, because I have dark hair and pale skin. I tell him that I danced for a dwarf the same night, that it was so cute. The dwarf wanted to fuck me, that part was less cute. My mother's ears are getting a perm. I stretched a ligament in my foot this week. I have to dance in cowboy boots. Tough week. My wallet's ego hurts so much that its zipper broke just now as I was about to pay at the Brûlerie. What do I do with my life? I write books, monsieur. Books that everyone can understand. Yes, a bit like *Twilight* but better, more poetic, let's say. I have pale skin, I'm a vampire, it's required. No, they're not pop psychology. The parents of the boy with the eel are psychologists. No, he's not my boyfriend. No, he doesn't love me. Yes, I'm hung up. He's the man of my life, monsieur, I'm just not the woman of his. The driver tells me to drop the "monsieur," he's going to get me to dance. We arrive at the IGA. I have to turn right, then run straight to the back. Meow, piano.

STANISLAS

You don't meow for anyone now. I don't give a shit about your private journal.doc. I'd like to react.doc but I won't. I'll criticize you. I'll tell you what you really are and everyone will listen to me because I'm still alive. You say that you're no one and everyone all at once, to be cute, but in actual fact, you're nothing. You're pus, that's what you are. Pus that rots away the words and all of literature. This is how it is. Accept it.

FUCK MEOW HARDER.DOC

I'm a whore. I'm playing the whore this week. No choice, too many expenses, and then this whole thing with the eel. But there are no eels here. He won't want me. I'm worthless without the eel. Meow. I buy two jars of whelks in vinegar. They come from Baie-Comeau, they're shellfish. Bathing in a whitish liquid. I'm going to have to buy more batteries for my dildo. I'll put the jar on a table in my bedroom. I'm going to have to masturbate thinking about the whitish liquid in the jar.

51

Nothing's changed. I'm just more of a whore than last month. Piano. I would totally bring you a jar of whelks to watch you suck them, but this man is coming over to "tune my piano." I arch my back just as I should and write this poem:

I drink two-dollar lemonade
and I love you
fuck meow harder
so I drip
a little

I close my eyes, I open my eyes.
The bird.
I call Dr. Boutiller The Bird.
He's nice.
He takes my hand.
I blink.
The Decadron makes my face swell and my eyes blink.
To give you an idea.
Yesterday my pillow was all kinds of things.
It started out as a cat.
Then, a dog.
When I opened my eyes, I saw.
It was a pillow the whole time.
I'm still at Notre-Dame.
My dinner will be here soon.
I'll sit on the chair.
I'll be a magician.
My ass is a dove.
I'll make it disappear.

To Raphaëlle, I bequeath:
this text for Thomas,
the babydoll she lent me
and one hundred fennec foxes.

RAPHAËLLE

We were friends. We knew each other from high school.
I set my alarm for five a.m. to go to work. She was leaving her job at that time. Different rhythms of life. Mathieu sent me a brown envelope full of black clothes that
I'd loaned her. I found this text on a key in the pocket of
my jacket. I always know what to wear but never what
to say. She was the one who knew what to say. I'm only
good at copy-pasting. At understanding the intensity, but
not at writing it.

THOMAS HILFIGER.DOC

I have another friend who committed suicide. I have a
friend who just died. I have a friend who just took his life.
These words fall onto the pavement. Thomas died today.
You think, but you don't think. These sentences, when
it's your friend saying them to you on the telephone,
it wasn't too bad, it hit hard, it hurt, but they were still

nothing but sentences. You don't know what to say, no-body ever knows what to say, you have nothing to say, you know that you don't have to say anything, but you try, you start a sentence—

I can't believe that,

I wonder how his mother can,

I remember that night in his parents' basement, the time that,

I remember the website he'd made to write about his two years travelling in China, where he'd talked about me, about how fun I was, and creative, and how much he was going to miss me,

I remember having read his Facebook status updates, that they'd made me smile, that he'd seemed like he was blossoming,

—you manage to compile a list of memories, but you know that you're already beginning to forget them, you're angry at yourself, at your goldfish memory, you're angry to have stopped writing to him, two years ago already. You wonder if you would have been able to change something, if you would have known how to find the right words, heal a wound here and there, you wonder if you could have postponed this act. You tell yourself that you could have called him, that you could have asked for his number, called him once in a while. You tell yourself that you could have called him that very day, surprised him, told him something nice, something simple and sincere. You wonder if that could have had some small effect.

RAPHAËLLE

Her headphones didn't do it for her. She was a girl made for speakers. I'd loaned her mine, the black headphones, they're in the brown envelope. I wonder if her earwax will mix with mine. I wonder if her ears are still producing wax. I could call The Parakeets or The Bird to ask them. I could ask everyone except her. She's dead. The Parakeets was her speech therapist at the hospital. The Bird was her neurosurgeon, the one who couldn't do anything. When she was a kid, she had two parakeets, Marie and Stéphane. It was Marie-Stéphane's fault if they always forgot to put tea on her tray. Her neurosurgeon had a bird haircut. Dishevelled. Like greasy feathers, silky chips.

THOMAS HILFIGER.DOC

My condolences to his family, my condolences to his closest friends, my condolences. My condolences to his mother, his father, his brothers and sisters, his girlfriend, everyone who loved him, who knew him, everyone who spent even just one night with him. My condolences. I have to find a way to get motivated, I have to go to work, I have to. I have to because tomorrow I need to buy flowers, a big arrangement of flowers, flowers that I'll choose myself, that I'll arrange myself. I have to go to work, I have to put on shiny panties and huge stilettos and go to work, go shake my fringe, go seduce men and take all their money. I wouldn't have anything better to do if I stayed at home. I wouldn't have a cent, just half a pack of cigarettes and the desire to drink like never before, to allow myself to cry, to take hold of the feeling. And I couldn't stay here, at my place, mine that I share with Jackie and Alice and Carl and Patrick and his Anglophone friend whose name I can't remember. I couldn't take their strident voices and their drunken laughter, I couldn't take the contrast between myself and the others. At least at work I can cuddle up in this overblown image of myself, I can play the star dancer, the super sex bomb. The mischievous, the saucy, the in-a-naughty-mood. And make money, to buy flowers, to go, to find the courage to go to the funeral home.

RAPHAËLLE

I didn't go pay my dollar of existence to his family. She didn't either. We stayed rich, each at our homes. Family, I owe you two bucks. I owe money almost everywhere. Loonies here and there. I went to find her with her wheelchair. I got her out of her robe. She drooled everywhere. It was disgusting. If I were a bird, I would stand beneath her mouth. Disgusting, but full of nutrients. Leftovers from yesterday's gratin, streams of coffee, drool. An organic shower for ravenous birds. She didn't want to see Max in his black box. She wanted to go into the other room. I didn't understand at first, I followed her, I understood.

THOMAS HILFIGER.DOC

It's crazy what your brain does in these kinds of situations. When someone asks you a question, there's a little hand inside your head that will immediately push aside the right curtain and grab some good material to share. When someone tells you that someone you knew is dead, you have no more resources, you have eight little hands, the medusa in your head, all your thoughts solidify, the curtains fall, you are naked in a desert of concrete and gyprock and you can't stop repeating to yourself: You must react, how to react, r.e.a.c.t. You rummage through your memories, you manage only to remember useless details, insipid moments, the places you spent your nights, the things your friend told you about him, the time you'd all watched a movie in his parents' basement, his parents' kitchen all done in wood, you simply cannot summon a memory of him, you never will again, it's as if he'd already begun dying way earlier. You remember his face the time you talked to him on the balcony but you can't remember his hands, his proportions, you can't recall the sweater he wore all the time. You remember that he'd written to you, but you don't remember anymore what it was and that makes you angry. But what makes you even angrier is that you remember very well that the message was full of mistakes and it had irritated you. It makes you angry that you always prioritize the negative in the order of information, always and especially now. It's not the time to think of these things, it's the time to think nostalgically of good times, of bad, but not of the ordinary.

RAPHAËLLE

The boy in the black box, the black urn, they explained to me, he was also named Stanislas and he died of brain cancer. The black urn. It was better that way. He would always be thirty-one. His brain was an unhappy Care Bear. Like Vickie's. That day, the rainbow that shone out of his shitty asshole almost didn't fade. That day, Vickie had a bulging eye. She was macabre and ruined. Completely white. Like a blank page. Stanislas had a complicated last name. Something Russian or Slovak. The foxes came into the building, I didn't open the door for them. The voice of Caprice and her shrill cunt stories. I'm happy that that girl's far away from us in the hallway of the funeral home. Someone to look after the animals. The foxes will end up being shriller than her cunt. Soon we'll leave in the darkness. We'll hold Vickie's hands in the meantime. Vickie will end up being shriller than anyone in her silence. By day, you can penetrate people with silent contemplation. By night, in this case. Vickie wanted to wear black to walk with the night. That's what she said. She was always such a big liar.

THOMAS HILFIGER.DOC

It's crazy, the things that are upsetting. We forced ourselves, we are still and always forcing ourselves, non-stop, to find interesting things to do, to live the big moments, big nights, big and open conversations, the epic, and in the end, it's the simplest moments that shine through, the most banal, often just moments of silence, moments of just being in the same room as that person, doing something that doesn't require talking, or requires very little, sometimes a few words, a question, but never the response. You remember more of yourself with him than of him with you. You remember what you were wearing when you went out, but you don't remember the bar, or who was there or what happened, just that your American Apparel dress looked really good that night. Then it flips, you remember that you'd stolen that dress, and from which location, Mont-Royal, that it was a chilly night and that you'd walked down the alleyway after leaving the store because you were afraid of getting caught and that an employee would be following you down the street. You don't understand what you're doing, thinking about American Apparel at a time like this. It's not like if you could pull yourself together, if you could think better the next time – we only die once. Apparently when your friends die, you're only able to think about a stupid American Apparel dress and how you got it. You tell yourself that you should have begun to feel sad and cry a good twenty minutes ago, but it's not like that can happen on command, and this is not the time to fake it. All of this comes from the purest sincerity. Clothes and clothes, it always comes back to clothes. It's heartbreaking.

RAPHAËLLE

I'm wearing a black dress. Vickie too. We're wearing black. I think black is charming. It's slimming. For her, it was more complicated. Everything was always more complicated. She did so many things at once, said and cried so many things at once. It was the festival of mourning, of exclamation points. She looked at the urn and promised the lady she'd stop smoking. Too much death. She's like the sick people on the packages. Frail and yellow. Urea, nicotine, clearly. To dry, to crumble, to smoke. She was no longer a girl. She was a fragment. A little amalgam of over-seasoned flesh.

THOMAS HILFIGER.DOC

You tell yourself it isn't worth it to cancel your shift to grieve because you don't really see this grief coming. You tell yourself that you'll find the drive to get motivated and to go exhaust yourself in this uncertain feeling. You make up your mind, you'll go to work. You get up, you put on your stilettos and your backpack, you decide to walk to the club, to think a little, and then you go in, you get undressed, you're the first one on the floor. An hour passes, not a soul, two hours pass, one soul, forty dollars. You're sitting on a bench next to the DJ booth and you can't stop looking at yourself in the mirror, finding yourself ugly, noticing that your hair looks greasy, you pull it up in a ponytail, you braid it, you undo the braid, you sweep it to the side, you go downstairs to your dressing room and put on a little hairspray, you go back up, perch on another bench, and it's the same choreography, rewind, play, over and over. Suddenly you can't lie to yourself any longer, you have greasy hair, you're not pretty today, you are a sexual zero today, your friend died today, there's no money to make here. You freak out. You do your little act, you go see the boss, walking toward his office you think how you'll have to make something up in order to leave earlier, that you're on the rag, that you have bad cramps, but you don't really want to lie to him either. You tell him that there's no money to be made here and you don't want the money enough anyway to keep up this hair choreography all night. He tells you to never come back to his bar, you say thank you and go home. When you climb the stairs to your apartment and hear a concerto of voices through the door, you say fuck and go inside.

RAPHAËLLE

Isabelle had cut her hair and her mother had done her armpits and eyebrows. I'm wearing my brooch. The series recreates itself.

THOMAS HILFIGER.DOC

It's the G21 in your apartment, there are more people than chairs. The neighbour calls to complain. That lousy second-last Daft Punk record is playing again and everyone's drunk, everyone's talking loudly, Jackie is shrieking, Alice tells you she loves you. You tell yourself that everything's not over, that you can sit down on a chair, you have the right to claim one, you pay the rent to be able to sit on a chair in your apartment whenever you want. You still can't manage to concentrate on your grief. You start sewing feathers onto your corset for your Halloween costume. Always with the clothes, always these post-adolescents busy drinking beer and fucking everything up in your apartment, you can't listen to them talking anymore, always seeing the flaws and weaknesses in their conversations, but you never say anything, you suck it up and sew your feathers, and you smoke one cigarette after another, your eyes sting but you still don't cry. Don't want to talk about it.

RAPHAËLLE

Jackie and Alice arrived. Caprice dragged her new boy-friend along. She introduces him to Jackie and Alice. The foxes were annoyed. Vickie never meets the kind of boy who does everything for the girl he loves, like in the movies. She put the film in backwards. She woke up without her clothes in a bathtub near the Cadillac metro. She'd been lied to, drugged, robbed. There are some things for which panties are just decorative. I put my camera in its case, I take a photo of my camera in its case with my cell phone. I send it to the Musée d'art contemporain. In my dreams. I prefer the sticky drool that hangs from Vickie's mouth to the complete sentence. I'll wipe her mouth, even if she hates that.

THOMAS HILFIGER.DOC

Tommy and his co-worker Magella show up with a tiny bottle of rum and things to say. You don't know them, you meet them. You talk a little. You learn that nobody knows the Anglophone Mexican guy sitting at the other end of the table, that Alice's boyfriend met him on the street and decided to bring him along. The Mexican guy has the eyes of a killer or a rapist, you get paranoid, it gives you a little something to be dramatic about, you tell yourself that you could go through fear to get to grief, but it's in vain. Nothing works. Jackie does her flirty little tease routine, as usual; there are guys around, so something clicks in her ditzy little brain. She stands on her chair and shows her ass. She tells stories about being naked and drunk in places where you'd also been, stories that you've heard a thousand times too many because you were also there fifty percent of the time. She shouts, she talks about music with Magella, she knows everything, she knows all about music, she interrupts everyone to share this knowledge that you've heard her spill again once again one thousand times too many because you already knew it all. You're sick of hearing it. You say to yourself: Get your clothes on, get out of this smelly apartment, go to L'Esco, drink a beer and think. So you put on your coat. Tommy and Magella were having fun chatting with you, they tell you they'll come join you there after their last drink. Jackie shrieks meeee tooooo, you think fuck, you hope she passes out on the table, you'd like to knock her out, but that's just it, the problem, she's already basically out for the count. Wanting to marry rich men and not being able to, that's her drama. You don't want that to be yours, but you live with it, she's up your ass and shaking her own in your face all the time. Now you're outside. Now you're at L'Esco. Still no grief, still with the clothes. You check out what people are wearing in the bar, you think how that's the only thing you're able to remember, so you meticulously note all the buttons on all the jackets and all the belts of all the pants, tattoos of cat paws on breasts, glasses with no glass, leather boots. Jackie and the others arrive, you have a feeling that Jackie's going to touch her breasts in public, and you feel like Monday, Tuesday, Wednesday, like every day. Tuesday, Thomas died, Jackie was touching her breasts in public, I bought myself a two-foot rose to boost my morale. Outside. Cigarette. Everyone follows. You talk with Tommy. You think his name is Thomas because your brain is winking at you, but you only notice this later, so you never call him by his name. You don't want it to hurt. It sucks when it hurts in public and you might as well touch your breasts too like a girl gone wild for all that would do. Last call. You slam back your drink. You go back to your place with Tommy and Jackie. You "borrow" a dozen beer from Alice and Patrick, you leave them a twenty on the bedside table. Jackie wants to watch *Toy Story 3*, you put on *Toy Story 3*, you don't watch it, she falls asleep, you talk. You talk all night and it feels good to talk. Thomas-Tommy is interesting, he lived on the street, he doesn't seem like a junkie, he wasn't one, it figures. I find him sexy and I kind of want him, but I don't want to think about it. There's a girlfriend at his house sleeping all alone in their big bed. Normally, you don't give a shit about morals, but you think that you can't not give a shit today, it would be too many things to deal with at once. Still no grief. Thomas-Tommy leaves. You fall asleep proud of yourself.

RAPHAËLLE

I'll go by and see her tomorrow. Her new hobby: pacing along the walls. Someone has to be there to interpret the silences in the other rooms. She's there to interpret. I just read. Outside of myself, I read. So many painful reasonings, so many magnetic resonances. It sounds almost the same, but it's completely different. The resonating takes place in a huge machine. The reasoning doesn't take place at all. There's no machine for that. It doesn't exist yet. It would have to be a machine with a bunch of arms and metal chains. It would have to be just for me. A single serial number and my hand to write it down. No calm, no expression on my face.

THOMAS HILFIGER.DOC

You wake up from one of the best, one of the worst wet dreams of your life the next afternoon. He was there and you jumped on each other in secret. He had a cock that was eight inches long and three inches wide, and he was a fucking great kisser and God, the sex was good, you're still vibrating from it when you wake up. All this makes you angry because it's not possible. Someone is dead, someone you knew is dead and it doesn't stop you from going out for a beer with friends, it doesn't stop you from having an impossible wet dream where there's a guy with a fucking watermelon for a penis. You say to yourself how when you die you'd like it if people couldn't do things like that, for it to have more of an effect on them. You want, you really want to be able to be a good example, but you can't. You're sad, but not sad enough. The one who died, you never knew him too well, you just kind of knew who he was. The lack of substance of this relationship stops you from having any real emotions, a real sadness, from experiencing a real grief. All you can do is offer your condolences to his family. Buy flowers, say "my condolences," and take people in your arms as needed. But when you think of it, you tell yourself that if someone in your circle was to die and only tons of unknown faces came to perform this little number for you, it would just end up making you angry, it would be insulting that nobody shared your pain, your loss, your distress. It would be insulting that they showed up with beer breath and a hard cock in their eyes.

RAPHAËLLE

I emptied out the contents of the brown envelope. Clothes, black headphones, friends. A hundred fennec foxes for each one. The friend is dead. Her friends, too.

THOMAS HILFIGER.DOC

Thomas wrapped a zip tie around his neck. At that moment, on my computer, Uffie was strolling through her YouTube video, pushing doors and extras out of her way. Thomas hung himself with the zip tie around his neck. On my computer, I was writing: Ryan Gosling is so sexy. Thomas dead, waiting for someone to discover his body, and at that moment I was buying big white feathers, a white tutu and a mask for my swan costume in a store on avenue Mont-Royal. Always back to the clothes. And then always these contrasts, always this makeup. Such is my drama: always caught up again in the vulgarities of life, early or late, if not today then tomorrow, if not right away then soon. I will never be able to write beautiful love stories, never with any ease, anyway. I will always have to push doors and extras out of my way, cry wolf, and on top of all that, whine and dramatize it all.

I close my eyes, I open my eyes.
My liver still aches.
I close my eyes, I open my eyes.
I'm twenty-three. Why does my liver ache?
I close my eyes, I open my eyes.
I'm dizzy. My heart is beating way too slowly.
I close my eyes, I open my eyes.
My body is still scrap.
I wonder what it would be like, to die, or what it would
    be like to come within a hair's breadth of it.
I imagine stop-motion to the telephone, just before—
Like that.
In my mother's living room.
I close my eyes, I open my eyes.
My bottle of water is empty. Two sips left.
Two bars left on the battery of this life.
Really not cool.
I burp, what the fuck.
Maybe I'm reacting to the chili, after-dinner nap.
I close my eyes, I open my eyes.
It feels like a full day has passed every time I open
    my eyes.
It's all mixed up, it's contradictory.
It's like I was waking up and falling asleep at the
    same time.
Oreo, three.
White sleep.
I close my eyes and I keep them closed a long time.

To Catherine, I bequeath:
this text,
my inflatable doll
and one hundred fennec foxes.

CATHERINE

She drank ginger pear tea. I'm drinking wine. I went to her party and she died. She was twenty-three and I was there, with wine again. Twenty-three forever. I imagine my own death sometimes, too. In not so long. I'm going to drink way too much wine. I'm going to miss her. I'll kiss guys and girls for her. Sing karaoke for her. I'll talk about her all night, drinking wine. The envelope Mathieu sent me is brown, nut brown. It reminds me of the flavoured coffee I accidentally ordered in the university cafeteria. Back when there were still schools. I'm much better off with wine. The coffee wasn't drinkable. Vickie listened to me tell that story even though it's boring. It's my turn to listen to her. I look at the brown envelope on my kitchen counter. I'll open it, and I'll find Vickie annoying. Injustice. Twenty-three. A usb key. A document.

Smoking ages you. It's like I'm constantly smoking the same cigarette. The cigarette never changes. It's me that changed. It's always the same brown, the filter always the same yellow. Always the same grainy hue. My mouth doesn't pick up much. A few illnesses. That's all. It seems like I should always be changing the subject. But I am the subject. Say something interesting. Jump high. Uniform attention. With the little gold star for style. My legs hurt. I'm whining. I have a vagina, so I whine. That's how it is. The subject: uninteresting. Mathieu says that's the reader's problem. They're the ones who choose. Mathieu might be right. But I want to tell you that you're beautiful, reader. I'm nice like that.

CATHERINE

The envelope has a strange shape. It's in a pile on my counter. Just next to the fruit bowl. An old apple is dying there. I wonder how old it is. I'm listening to dubstep. Vickie loved dubstep. She always wrote with music on in the background. I'm kind of obligated to listen to dubstep while I read, in homage. Féérique doesn't like it. Féérique is my daughter and I know how old she is, and she's not twenty-three. I wonder if Mathieu could send a brown envelope to Féérique when it's my turn to die. There's no return address on the envelope I received, Mathieu's work is done. There'll be more than one document, that's for sure. I tear open the envelope. The shape that I felt, it was an inflatable doll. I just had a cigarette,

I'll wait a little. I wouldn't want to give lung cancer to Inflatable Vickie.

JEAN SHORT PARTY.DOC

It's distressing, heartbreaking, crazy hard to watch yourself operating the heavy machinery that is the French language with hands that are all thumbs. I'm in a suit, my hair in a bun, but I'm still not employable. Take note. I'm in a dull-coloured suit, like the office. I'm wearing office colours because I'm working in my office. It's not a nice sentence to think or to live. What mess have I landed myself in? What great shame? I have to return my movies. They're all over the floor. I didn't watch a single one, that's the kind of attention span I have. I light another cigarette to pretend I'm doing something.

CATHERINE

It makes me want to smoke a million cigarettes. Me too, I want to pretend. It's like an old movie.doc. Back when there were still schools. Back when they took the time to teach us that cigarettes are bad, that they'll kill us. The doll is blown up. Vickie wrote her name on the forehead of her double: Inflatable Vickie. So that we understand that it's her double. Féérique asks questions, I don't answer. It's bugging me. Vickie's living hand wrote her own name. She knew she was going to die. She didn't say a word. We wouldn't have listened. Better safe than sorry, fille. You should have said something. We would have drunk wine together and talked about it. I would have stroked your hair. You're the only one I ever call honey. You were. We would have improvised that girls' night that we'd promised to do. I would have done your hair in two braids. I know how to braid. I have a little girl. I'll pour you a drink. Drink up, doll. It's like water, but better.

JEAN SHORT PARTY.DOC

The night you came back from Victo, I had a dream that you were hit with a stray bullet and lost an eye, and I was reading to you in your hospital room. I would read to you for the rest of my life, Stanislas. It would make me happy. I recorded all of Woolf's *The Waves* for you, just in case. I listened to a little of it. Carillon in the throat. I wasn't able to get through the whole thing. I squeezed my glass of strong wine so hard I almost gave myself a nosebleed. I wouldn't have felt a thing. My face was hungry, but I ignored it. I haven't eaten anything since my niçoise salad. It's a tough act to follow. Everything I write is about this boy. He's a tough act to follow. I'm excited for all that to be over. Being sad is boring. Tell your left eye that it's pretty. I text you silly things because I'm sad. I'm allowed, I tell myself. I'm completely naked underneath my skirt. I'm always completely naked. I'm naked in overalls and I'm topless in jeans. Just one piece to slip off and I'm naked. I'm a simple .doc. You can let me carry out my updates while you work. But you don't work.

Poor Stanislas. Poor Mathieu. Poor little, melancholic girl. I remember that she'd talked about it on her blog, about that dream. Nobody commented. It's too late to do it now. I wonder if Mathieu manages her email addresses, too. Maybe there's an automatic reply. Something like "Dude, I'm dead." I hope that Shawn loved her, he was her only real official boyfriend. I could go to the video store, but I'm too comfortable here. I'll find girly movies on the Internet. I always cry over cartoons.

JEAN SHORT PARTY.DOC

We are enfants terribles. We are absent sons. We are of the same boring family name. We are boring history. We are not even worthy of mention. We are in your playlist either way. We are not far from many other important names. We are missing the point. We are not full of gentle slopes. We are abrupt. We are Rocky Road. We are ice cream and we get eaten. We get swallowed and then we spin. We are yet to be announced. We are the enfants of the revolution. We are not even yet fully born. We are as dead as we are living. We walk a straight line. We fall from on high. We never conquered. We failed.

CATHERINE

We have the same last name. Had. That's what she should have written on the face of Inflatable Vickie, our last name. Féérique fell asleep super quickly. Her memory of the movie will be vague and all mixed up. She'll think that it's the story of a gang of stars and a mountain. Vickie would have remembered it in full, and it would have taken her three tomes to retell it. She would have hired a graphic designer. She would have made a million parentheses. She always had something to say, to add, a paragraph to insert. Always the need, the urgency to embellish. Trouble turned tirelessly around the little pole at the centre of her hand. She would have finished her glass of wine. I'll drink it in her place. I have to forget. The apocalypse outside, I have to forget it. The glass of wine she didn't finish, I can't ever forget that.

JEAN SHORT PARTY.DOC

As we fail, a good woman gives us refuge. It's such a cold attitude that the windshield wipers need imagination to work. I'm a car. I cry bolts. I don't have enough gas to go die in the middle of the highway. A shitty car, super cheap. A topless, cheap car. Catherine had a car accident. Samson told Heidy about it. Heidy didn't even know the names of the people who were in the car with Catherine. I feel like a car that's a bit jealous. This is ridiculous. Heidy has the right to know more names than me. Heidy's a DJ, she mixes in a tutu, everyone wants to be her friend. Me, I write topless. Writing is boring. I wear cowboy boots to get around. I should have become a DJ, I have two tutus. Fuck, it's boring, writing. You stink all alone in your corner. You're always on the rag. Nobody wants to talk to you, nobody wants to fuck you. You stink and you sleep alone all the time. I'd like to have never begun writing. Yesterday, you were out in real life with people and you wore boots.

There are cowboy boots in the entrance, vestiges of an unoriginal Hallowe'en. I'll put them on Inflatable Vickie. I don't have a tutu, but it's too late anyway, her life is over. We'll go somewhere, on foot. I don't know where yet. There's not enough wine here. I drank her glass in one gulp. I'm happy I'm friends with the guy at the dépanneur. He'll think I'm sketchy, coming in with my doll. One night, Vickie had told him that she was sad because of a boy. I could tell him she's dead. He liked her too. He'll want me to leave him the doll so he can make use of in it the conventional way. Vickie was pretty. Was, yes. Verb tenses are difficult in times of grief. Everyone wanted to fuck her. No matter what she says in that text she gave me. Why is she telling me about that night? I remember that I had an accident. I know quite well that I could have died, but she's the one who's dead. I know how it ends.doc. Vickie dies, I receive a brown envelope from Mathieu, I talk to a doll, I put boots on it and take it to the dépanneur.

JEAN SHORT PARTY.DOC

You were selling beer at a party, to help your friends out. You were wearing sequins. Everyone wanted to be your friend. It was a filmmaker party, but they didn't want to talk about film. You left. People never want to talk about film at parties like that. Maybe if I'd been topless, people would have wanted to talk about film with me. I didn't dare. I should have. I should have written to Catherine to ask her about the news, too. But I'm afraid that she's the one, the new girl that Stanislas is seeing. He didn't want to answer when I asked him if she was wearing a braid to make some kind of witty joke in the address book of my phone. It's sketchy. It's ridiculous and sketchy. Maybe wearing my jealousy suits me better. Too much skin, too much beige. The shame is palpable. Children are dying. I'm topless. Waves break on the shore. We are enfants terribles. We fall asleep topless and empty.

I can type with my eyes closed.
I learned how to type in one month in high school.
I was a secretary, I often did dictations.
I close my eyes.
My hands are beaks and my body is multicoloured.
My liver is blue, green, turquoise.
I open my eyes. I am beige and boring.
Never mind.
I have a subconsciousness full of feathers and a
    consciousness all in tatters.
I can type with my eyes closed, but my telephone is in
    my red bag.
I close my eyes anyway.
I play with my right nipple, my liver isn't far.
My hand feels weird.
It reminds me of my accident with the filet mignon, my
    burnt hand, the bandage.
That's the hand I support my whole body with when I
    turn around the pole.
I open my eyes.
I'm heavy.
I manage quite well with just my head, my hands, my
    right nipple, my heart and my vagina.
I know there are a bunch of other organs.
I look at the ceiling.
I'm dizzy.
That's cream, that's sand, the nuances multiply.
It makes me want to eat an oatmeal cookie and go pee.
A girl's skin is being bruised by a man in a van
    somewhere.

My father types with one hand.
Me too, when I only have one hand.
My lunch is supposed to arrive soon.
I'll email my mother.
I'm too vegged out to get up.

To Mikka, I bequeath:
this poem,
the salmon in the dumpster
and one hundred fennec foxes.

MIKKA

The car that took her to the end was neither red nor mine. It was yellow, and it made a lot of noise but not at all electro. Mathieu says that it was literature that gave her the tumour. Maybe. Her life was going so well. I was angry when I read that poem of hers. I had an idyllic romance with that girl. The dead girl, Vickie. I liked her a lot, but she told me too many secrets too quickly, it frightened me. She wrote a play. There will be a big red car in the background of the stage, somewhere behind the actors. Frederique is a theatre girl, too. I love theatre girls.

SAMANTHA FUCKS.DOC

a perfect gentleman
you go hide in your bedroom
to shuck your corn
you rent a motel room

to shuck your corn
your pillow wriggles
the sequins on my sweater exploded
you flew off
the sheets are milky
the bed stoned with desire
foam of so many legs
intoxicated floors
that we pay for

MIKKA

Every time I see a red Tercel, I think of her. Of her, naked. Naked in those hotel rooms she paid for with the
ass I'd come fuck her in. I'll always remember that night
with her at the Pomerol, a hotel downtown. She'd been
raped in Abitibi. She told me everything, only me. The
room at the Pomerol was at the end of the hallway. Like
Red Car's room in Abitibi. I left her there. With Red Car
at the end of the hallway. In her. Maybe I should have
stayed. I was such a coward. At least, now, I can share her
secret. Now that she's no longer here to cry like a fox.

SAMANTHA FUCKS.DOC

snow
i make an angel
made a star
gratis
the maid knocks
i'm rabid
yellow skin

sweet urea
i have slippery wings
you left silent as a priest
the bed is still warm
the bird came in
through the closed windows
through the curtains that teleport
sprung from a pattern
the mascara is calling me
i find your package of cigarettes
forgotten in the bathroom

MIKKA

Red Car thrums at the back of the stage. Little sounds of suffocating foxes. Crusty Old Car. With stroboscope eyes. The night of the Pomerol, we were supposed to make a little dinner at her friends' place, I was going to meet her at Station Centrale and head over. She wanted to make us crusted salmon. Mission abandoned. The night of the Pomerol, she only wanted to cry in the shower. She told me everything at once, the recipe, the ingredients, the events of the day before, or at least what little she could remember. It was all mixed up. But it was mainly that life goes on, went on. The night of the Pomerol, I left without saying why. A salmon rotted for her that night in a dumpster somewhere. Poor girl. She is always one fish away from love. Poor girl and poor foxes, suffocating and crying. Maybe it was in that Abitibi loft that this tumour really set in. That's where she was raped. It had to happen. It was going to happen. It happened. I told myself that she was doing too well for it to last. Something had to go wrong. I said nothing, it was better that way. I would have had the weight of the world on my back. It has to be for that reason that I'm at the end of the book. She talked to me about that epic scene in *Storytelling*, the Solondz film, where one of the authors says that she'd like to have been raped so that she would have a trauma from her youth to work with. The motor sputters and I said nothing. I went with her. I held her hand while she took a shower. She knew I was freaking out. My hand was boiling. I was lobster red and completely broken by the world.

SAMANTHA FUCKS.DOC

bathroom haiku
full of a spider's starry drool
i have eight hands
i miss having four
you left a note on the flap of the package
i peeled off the liquid paper between your lines
i fed my duck
a poem
unreadable
one word per line
there are too many parking lots
inhumane traffic
room for nobody
total waste
you forgot a digit in your number
your bottle of medicine

empty
on the counter

MIKKA

I left her alone with her fear. There was no hopscotch game drawn on the sidewalk. Life was hard. To be a woman of her generation: hard. Every time I step on a crack, a fox coughs. I live far away, but I walked anyway to think. She begged me to make love to her. Everything's been dark inside me ever since. I left, I shut the door gently behind me. I left her alone in that room. I should have stayed.

SAMANTHA FUCKS.DOC

the broken doorbell?
the fur rug at the foot of the door
for the whole world
from fully-equipped murderer to sensitive little poet
peel up the rug
the bone key
not a cent for the bus
towards the telephone
a vulture makes his nest in my uterus
you hid our first kiss
beneath the foot of your cup of red wine
you hid your smoke in the ashtray
the sky drank a little beer
the clouds took a little piss
the bird goes to hide in the taxi
and i follow

I didn't stay in that room. It was like I'd left without paying. She felt bad. She wrote to me later. I responded, told her not to love me anymore, then I rolled over: Frédérique was looking more beautiful than usual and she hadn't been raped.

SAMANTHA FUCKS.DOC

forgot to pick up
your cigarette butts outside
want to put
Tide in my ideas
Bounce in my plans
i'm breakable today
crystal
to fill with champagne
pixelated face
of dry ice
today
don't want to cry
yesterday
the bird shit in my glass
it's empty
and in the cabinet
people get me drunk
the garden is full of butts
to ash the lungs of the party
i go into the kitchen
Corona
an old shallot rots behind

Corona
i drink the tongue hanging out of the eyes
to unwind
the pain of loving
loving
the cock in the sun
the perched apostrophe
the beak in the air
the pain of loving
loving
i'm coming back and i already don't know anymore how
to go back there
the skull as a tea bag
to crumble
nothing written for a week
wet paper

MIKKA

Frederique and I make love. She's willing. We turn off
the lights. Our eyes know each other. Our bodies, too. I
didn't have any energy left to revive the little girl crying
in her Dark Room. She said that she'd die without knowing love. She was right.

SAMANTHA FUCKS.DOC

me, i sing for nobody
nobody lines up for the bathroom
nobody dances
nobody flashes their tits
nobody throws their panties at me

nobody asks for my autograph
"With love,
for Nobody Davidson"
"With warmest regards,
for Nobody Tremblay"
"With affection,
for Nobody Gagnon"

MIKKA
She died. Nobody Gendreau died. Done, bye.

I close my eyes, I open my eyes.

A prayer for Madame Tardif.

The Bible.

Our little Kobe tome.

I never left the hospital.

I will never fully leave the hospital.

I come back every day for my radiation treatments.

I have this little coloured scarf and a ton of hats to hide the hair I'm losing.

I close my eyes, I open my eyes.

I'm in L.A.

All the women are stopping me in the street to ask where I bought my hat.

At the Giant Tiger in Montréal, madame.

I'd like to have a more glamorous answer.

Why is nobody speaking to me in English?

I'm in L.A.

You're beautiful, madame, with your long, silky hair.

My hair is shorter than yours.

My lashes are longer.

I close my eyes.

It tickles the world.

To Martine, my mother, I bequeath:
this monologue recited by a five-year-old girl,
my flowered bikini
and one hundred fennec foxes.

MAMAN

Hubert Aquin does his washing in the water of Vickie's tears. Her tears are clear, she hasn't worn makeup in ages. She's my daughter. I took care of my sick mother, my grandmother at the end of her life, and now my daughter. I'm a natural caretaker. All of these women had blue-green eyes, except Vickie. She has brown eyes, like her father. A fun way to wring out the tears that collect on washcloths is to give them a punch. Try it, it's relaxing. Five-year-old Vickie appears to me, wearing the same dress as the one in the photo on the fridge. She hands me a bikini. Her voice is twenty-three years old. The bikini is eighteen.

HELVETICA PROVENCHER.DOC

I take down my hair. I pick flowers to put in my hair, but then I change my mind. I don't look pretty with flowers in my hair. I'm not that kind of girl, and besides, I have flowers on my bikini. Maman, you said that I look like a butterfly in my dress. I got a butterfly tattoo just above my pelvis when I was twenty-one. The bathing suit hides some of it. Maman, I slept with a man for money. With a few men for money, with five, to be exact. Maman, I took down my hair. Maman, I eat hard knocks for breakfast. Maman, I drank every day for six years. Last Wednesday, I had six Moosehead to start. I had two shots of calvados to finish. I was moaning in a booth, I barely remember it. Intermission of Jameson. Maman, I bought a discounted vibrator on Boxing Day. The part that stimulates the clitoris is a rabbit. Remember how I loved rabbits when I was little? Maman, I can reach all the buttons on the vending machine now, but I don't button up all of mine. Maman, my vibrator is in the top drawer of my dresser, underneath the papers, don't be startled. I'm dead, don't feel bad, you have to clean up, I understand.

MAMAN

Hubert Aquin makes himself a tea. Marie Uguay puts on her tutu. François Villon, a tuxedo. I don't know who these people are, but my daughter says they're important writers. I get them dressed. They're coming with me, I'm going tanning. I don't have any tattoos, but it's almost the same thing. The bikini looks as good on me as it did on her. The apple didn't fall far from the tree. One night, I turned off the lights and called her into the kitchen. I turned on the lights and shouted: I'm a unicorn. I was holding a highlighter to my forehead. It was so cute she fell over.

Maman, men loved me with their hands like you love me with your heart. The first was named Michaël, he was twenty-four, he wanted to marry me. It was so sad. He did rectal searches at the airport. To pay me. He still lived with his parents. To pay me. He'd only had one girlfriend in his life. I did a good deed. You know how nice I am. But I charged him a lot. I bought you the wooden watch, it was your birthday. I can reach the fountains now, but I don't drink water anymore. Maman, I took off my dress and never put it back on. Everyone saw my butterfly. I wrapped my lips around a few penises. I lip-synched to sexy songs in the metro. Nobody heard. I had my headphones. I lip-synched, it was silent, I never took the metro again. I can't handle the incessant procession of people. All these men, so many clients. I spent the night outside because I'd lost my keys. I was cold. I thought I was going to die and that seemed fine. The boy didn't live far, he could have found me. I called you from a phone booth, I arrived at your place an hour later. I recharged my cell phone all morning. I called my booker. That's where it all started. The dicks, the sheets, the career as erection attendant. My booker was named Étienne. You should call him, tell him I'm dead. He'll be sad, he liked our chats. His is the only incoming call on my phone for months. You can call him Titi. It'll make him laugh. I used to make him laugh. He, at least, will never forget me. I should never have taken down my hair. I have trillions of unused condoms in the upper pocket of my black suitcase. I won't use them. Yes, I figured I'd get rid of them by whoring. But that's not what killed me, Maman. No. What killed me was loving.

MAMAN

I wonder if Hubert Aquin, François Villon and Marie Uguay were the types to go tanning, too. I didn't understand any of Vickie's book. Her friend Mathieu is going to help me make some sense of this document. This book is supposed to be for everybody. I am nobody and everybody at once. What a mother, what a daughter. Crazy daughter. I should have stroked my belly more often. It's as if I'd put too much parsley in everything. And all of a sudden, boom, a sledgehammer. My daughter is dead. I have to reread her book. I promised her I wouldn't forget. I'll try again. But first, I'll go into the kitchen and call her. I turn off the lights, I turn on the lights. Vickie? Vickie?

I have too many drinks.
I made a mess everywhere.
My eyes go off the road.
I don't have control over the muscles of my face
    anymore.
My gaze wanders without me.
It's like I'm stoned all the time.
My tutu is always more than one colour now.
Mathieu would have stared at the toast.
He always stares at the toast if he's there when I eat.
I'm always alone in the morning.
The Parakeets lent me a cracked mirror for my diction
    exercises.
Tomorrow, I'll dine with someone else's misfortune.
My smile is crooked, I have a cavity.
It mustn't be fun to be my mouth.
My hand isn't too bad.
Suddenly I have a sweet tooth.
Just now I woke up shaking like a chihuahua.
Definitely because of my nicotine patch.
I focus on the positive, the essential.
It's necessary.
I think about desserts all the time,
fields of desserts.
That's positive, essential.

To Antoine, my brother, I bequeath:
this text,
this *Terminator* cigarette case,
and one hundred fennec foxes.

BROTHER

You motherfucker, I'd shove my fist up your ass and wave bye-bye to your shoes. You hurt my sister. And she didn't tell me anything about how to find you. She knows I'd hurt you so bad. Our father would hurt you. Even if he spent four years not giving a shit about her, or about me, about us – he'd hurt you all the same. The reader would hurt you, too. Everyone would. No exceptions, no rules. Life isn't a playground anymore, not for you. I buy ice cream cones for the girls I think are pretty. I bring them to the marina, we lock eyes for so long we wouldn't miss a single lash falling. The sun sets, I score, I'm sixteen.

ALMOST SCHWARZENEGGER.DOC

I wish I'd never known pain. I wish I'd never opened my mouth, pronounced my first word, only good for walking, for getting walked all over. Never my open mouth, my dilated ears. I wish I was stupid and ugly, understanding nothing. I wish I'd been dead at twelve, an innocent brain, with toilet paper turning clockwise, cotton candy naïveté. I wish I'd never put on my first sweater. Never been cold. Never worn my first jacket, first tuque, first glove. But especially, my first hat. Never my first hat. I wish I'd never gone rollerblading, never put on my first Band-Aid. Never gotten wasted for the first time, never taken the first Tylenol, the first amphetamines, the first bite of junk food. Never taken my first steps in high heels, gotten my first blisters. Never the sleepless nights, the anxiety, insecurity. Never the others. Never myself. Never the people who think they know it all, never the people who think they know me. I wish I'd been someone else, somewhere else.

BROTHER

I imagine Vickie outside at the marina, telling me about it, confiding in me, and that's the beginning of the end for you. You start not feeling so hot. I have superpowers. Your skin turns mauve. Then your cock. Oh, your cock. She turns it into jerky. Your mouth floods with lava, your teeth burst out of your face. You shit from your eyes. Your fingernails explode. I'm the child soldier who isn't digesting his rainbow very well. I'm the wild child with sixteen thousand powers.

ALMOST SCHWARZENEGGER.DOC

I am this literature, the shameful literature, full of regrets. I have filthy eyelids from having closed my eyes too often, from having had to do it too often. The tar that's produced by this subdued lighting. Me, closed in on myself, head on the asphalt, a road sign on the soles of my shoes: Don't go there, cul-de-sac, I'm coming back, hold onto your Kodak. Stay with the simple things. Keep smoking ten hash joints a day if that's what does it for you. Keep buying ice cream cones at the Sainte-Agathe crèmerie for the beautiful girls you meet.

BROTHER

Vickie had me and my mom over for dinner before she went back to the hospital for the last time. We don't have the same mother, but they look alike. Vickie was saying that some mornings were particularly hard. To be wide awake at two in the morning after a night of maybe four hours sleep. Those mornings, she said she found it cute to reread my text messages. Go sister, you're tough. It's not true, this fucking cancer won't get you. Then she started talking about literature, about how important it is to read more than Anne Rice and shit. She showed me a video of a fox eating an apple, without the sound, and she put on that old *Romantic Saxophone HD* for the soundtrack. We talked about all kinds of stuff. Our racist grandmother in Montréal-Nord. Come on, this is not cool, move. One plus one equals fucking two. Sister, I'll never forget you.

ALMOST SCHWARZENEGGER.DOC

When you come home completely stoned, lie to your mother if you want. But never lie to yourself. Never stop singing, singing to yourself in the shower, in the street, while you're washing the dishes at your mother's restaurant. Never prostitute yourself intellectually. Don't talk bullshit to seem interesting. Be yourself. Big or small. Without makeup. With morning breath. The soul has no need of Colgate. Don't boast, don't pity yourself. Simple words, simple sounds, agreeing in gender and number with your difficult years. Don't be mainstream, or easy to please. You can hide in the kitchen all your life if you want. No need for social exhibitionism. No need to jump high to be noticed. Quality, not quantity. Be your own little private party, be your hand that rises, easy, all the time, on demand.

BROTHER

I'd hurt you so, so bad. My sister's no whore. She wasn't looking for it. It's not like in the movies. She was a stripper and she never said a word about it to me. You did what you did and she never said a word. She talked to me about foxes, episodes of *Magic Bus*. Fennec foxes eat scorpions. Our father had bought me a scorpion back when he loved me, back when I was still cute. Having a scorpion makes you a man. Sister, I'm Arnold, I govern California, and you drink mojitos while I crush vermin with my huge, authentic boots, *Commando*-style.

ALMOST SCHWARZENEGGER.DOC

Never the first dirty plate. Never the first slimy plug. To never have dipped my hands in soapy water and then never been able to take them out, to take me out, even with all the adverbs of the world, never clean. Never anything but this allegorical ostrich. Never noble. Never well, never well-told, never at ease. Never understood, understanding, comprehensible. I'm this punk, androgynous, animal literature. I feel like dry ice, the kind that smokes. I have floating ideas and frozen feet. I contemplate the poetry performance scene and my gaze gets lost in the details. I lower my eyes: a super close-up shot of the hair growing on my legs. I have that to shield me, at least. I've got a head full of kohl, a head full of baby crows. Never wisdom, never wrinkles. Always fucking with my head with pencils. Silicone love, fiction, lies. Swallow everything. Swallow everything down. I'd like to be able to edit their little show and cut everything I just saw on the stage. The young poets simulate orgasms, stuck to the mic, onomatopoeias of circumstance. I'm nowhere near an orgasm. Back to back, face to face, give yourselves a hand and change places. I have ideas full of syringes. The door to the bookstore opens a crack. Montréal bleeds and I write with its blood. This text is not 7-Up for the soul gone flat. It's grappa for a heart on the threshold of alcoholic coma.

BROTHER
Man, if I see the word rape pronounced by my sister one more time, I'm gonna explode. I plan on rereading her book. You're in deep shit.

I open my eyes.

I scored a prescription for sleeping pills.

This morning, I wrote poems.

I'm going to give them to Anna.

She likes my poetry.

I want to make her happy.

She brought me to Namur metro so that I'd feel pretty
    buying new clothes.

Value Village isn't what it used to be.

It's expensive and it's far away.

I miss the costume designer at the Monument-National.

I close my eyes, I open my eyes.

I'm Pantalone on stage.

I have a huge boomerang nose.

I close my eyes, I open my eyes.

I'm Ginette Reno in Aero.

I make chocolate bubbles.

I melt on centre stage.

It's soft, it makes me hot.

I close my eyes, I open my eyes.

Éric Lapointe gives me a private show.

But I'm not in the room.

It's weird.

He's wearing a brown shirt.

To Mathieu, I bequeath:
this book,
my Pikachu sock
and one hundred fennec foxes.

MATHIEU

A thousand foxes passing through the area each made a pile on the ground to form a satanic star. Directly in the middle: the brown envelope. It's the brown envelope that contains everything. Vickie always found me funny in a crop top. I'll put on my old Britney Spears T-shirt and let her laptop warm up my belly. I'm a brown car without a hood. Marie Uguay in a tutu, my dear friend, the most important one, had brain cancer. Virtually impossible to beat. The adverb here becomes a question of survival. It's sad, surviving. Marie Uguay in a tutu was greatly, undeniably my most important friend. When I left Notre-Dame the first time, there was a man in a wheelchair with an empty glass on the ground in front of him, he seemed to be begging for gravel, his neck was mashed, his body soft, minced. She was a bit like that at the end. Like that, but in a tutu. I can still hear her. She filmed herself. *Pute Moment*, it's an experimental film.

Sad red juice, bitter black juice. It was as if she wore high-waisted pants all the time. Super-tight pants. It was as if her brain hatched an egg. An egg not meant for frying. She spent her life drunk. At the end, she couldn't drink anymore. It was over, the escapades finished. On her laptop, there are a ton of lists, and this book.

List of exciting and crazy things I did when I was drunk

I pissed in a sink at Marilou's.
I took a sip of old Éphémère beer mixed with the ash of a joint.
I turned around a pole, pretending to be a pigeon.
I stole the boyfriends of a bunch of girls and slept with them.
I tied a guy to the pole at Red Light with my G-string and poured shots of Sour Puss on his Metallica T-shirt.

The list goes on for pages and pages. She'd told me about the thing with the G-string. It'd happened in the same town as the rape. I know that now. I had a feeling it was that town. She didn't want to talk about Val-d'Or anymore. It was so obvious. I have a lot to digest. My friend was raped, became a whore and died. Greatly? Undeniably? I look up at the sky, fingers raised in fuck you formation. It wasn't enough, to see her degrade herself like that? You had to kill her too? I have two hands and her computer on my belly.

You call yourself the intellectual equivalent of a biker chick. You wear mime underwear. You live nowhere. Dynasty zero. Punk GPS. You melt a marshmallow with your lighter to make pin-up butter. You make a big slab of it on the ground. You go buy postcards at the gift shop. Your address: Montréal, QC. You leave Bistro de Paris by the back door. This bar bores the shit out of you. A turd in high heels.

MATHIEU

Stop being nice, stop being beautiful. Stop taking care of everyone, force-feeding them drugs with a smile. Stop moving so urgently with such agility. Stop, gazelles. Be like me. Big goats with big tusks. Make a lot of noise like those big machines of yours, with your big feet in this big room. Be big. I'll make myself very small. I'll go curl up. Poets curl up. In her hollow cheeks. As the drugs dug deep furrows in her cheeks, you were all beautiful, huge and soft. I was already crying for her imminent death. Curled up so tiny in one of her sick cheeks.

ARE YOU THE ULTIMATE PAC-MAN.DOC

Rock-hard eyes with double-D dark circles, you attach the two straps of your bra with the elastic coming out of your sleeve. Black pencil silence, veins ballooning red from a helium gaze. You hallucinate: a shadow in a cape at the mouth of the alley. It whispers that your blood tastes like sangria.

The big ladies had taken off her IV. One of you must have irrigated her this morning. It's like she has a correction pen planted in her arm. The tube of a red pen. It's kind of like that. I'll correct with her blood. She's gone, so I can definitely leave with this pen. It's only her mother and me here. Her mother wouldn't know what to do with her blood. I puff up my cheeks, I'm alive and well. I'll keep going to parties. She'll keep crying in my ears, this question that kills: Are you the ultimate Pac-man? I'll twist my tears from top to bottom. My cheeks will be swollen.

ARE YOU THE ULTIMATE PAC-MAN.DOC

You, little poet at the event, pure Québécois de souche. You say over and over that you have a big dick. That you're like a black albino. But you only caulk the little holes, the lock, never the room. You fuck the whole world in the ears, the sockets of the eyes, but never the head. You never say anything of importance. You play touche-pipi with literature.

MATHIEU

I just want to write a few paragraphs every day, eat shepherd's pie, and then watch her Brakhage box set while writing more paragraphs. All these subjects that don't want to die. To master this pretentious writing like her, to lose myself, empty my bag of that which lifts my heart and smashes me to the ground for failing to have beautiful things to say about the beautiful things of life. I'm sick of reading these lousy verses where dude is talking about this nymph, that sex, so magical, unique, unbelievable, the best of your life, always the new best of your life. You get to the end of the collection with empty balls and sticky hands, but you're still hungry.

ARE YOU THE ULTIMATE PAC-MAN.DOC

You wrote a poem called "I am not an imposter" and everyone thinks you're being ironic when you read it.

MATHIEU

I have little, red cheeks. I'm a little person. I drank a coffee before coming to read her poem on stage. I'm the operator of her literature, I'm the one who manages it. I'm the one she asked to read. Are you the ultimate Pac-Man.doc? Her mother is crying somewhere and I'm here with this machinery in my hands and a thousand fennec foxes that follow me around everywhere. I came up here on this stage to read you this important question.

ARE YOU THE ULTIMATE PAC-MAN.DOC

Your whole family bought your book.

MATHIEU

Her whole family bought hers. Nobody understood it. This is the question you have to listen to, lovely mother, beautiful uncles. Are you? The ultimate? Pac-Man?

You, on ten generations to come.

MATHIEU

Her Celtic astrology said so. She was going to be posthumous. The queen is dead. She was so trashy, so sparkly, so explosive, so much of her generation. François Villon in a tuxedo, wrapped up in deleted themes. Love: to never speak enough of it, to speak of nothing but. Marie Uguay in a tutu. I know we loved her. Her friends, her mother, and me. So naked, so real, princess of nothingness.

ARE YOU THE ULTIMATE PAC-MAN.DOC

You, a stripper to the tips of your fingernails, you who begins a text but doesn't finish it, not right away, later, who lets it languish in that infinite purse that you're always nearly forgetting in the next day's coat check. You live in a gigantic, amorphous blue ball. The two dolphins of your lips do a triple jump in the hoops of your cheeks, but what goes up must come down. You wind up your face again, the music box, you listen to Sexy Sushi, you write: Am I better in tempura or sashimi? You're so literal.

MATHIEU

Nobody loved like she did. Nobody will ever love like her again. Love in Comic Sans, so that nobody will ever forget her.

Poems of five little verses. The Minigo of literature. Words spoken with a tongue sticking out, desirable and badly kissed. It'd be desirable to have eaten the wings of a barbequed turtledove for breakfast.

MATHIEU

Her mother had washed some blueberries. She won't be eating them. I stuff them into my cheeks like a squirrel with a mouthful of nuts.

ARE YOU THE ULTIMATE PAC-MAN.DOC

And to have served friends a buffet for dinner. Quail sautéed in maple butter, gerbil brains in wine sauce, spit-roasted baby seal, hippocampus spring rolls, kittens in vinegar, dragonfly chips, hamster dumplings and chihuahua skewers. To always make just one bite of everything. To eat with my eyes.

MATHIEU

I'm hungry, I drank a coffee, it's already too much. I'm a fragile, little animal. I'm shaking like a baby chihuahua on a skewer. Literature dinner: a shitload of Brussels sprouts and two or three medallions of pork. I want to be properly outraged. No need to keep searching, uselessly poring over books, so that they'll serve me columns of brown sauce, so that they'll organize me in notebooks. So that they'll tell me what to think: You are hungry. You must drink coffee. You must go to this event and read this text of your dead friend. This is how it is.

You, with a steamroller in one hand and a gel pencil in the other. And you, who pukes in your own mouth and who opens wide.

MATHIEU

Stop. The queen is dying. You're all running everywhere and I'm shrinking. All the foxes are crying in the hallways of Emergency. The cries come straight from their bellies. The belly of the beast crying out. Everyone hopes a poem, a little something. Stop. There'll be too many foxes. This fucking final moment. The end of a world. A world with her in it.

ARE YOU THE ULTIMATE PAC-MAN.DOC

Or even you, little poet in construction, Sico collection, dropping colours every ten words, a boy with luxurious green irises, rainbow ideas, you spend so much time on the interior decoration of your poem and barely two minutes on its excavation.

MATHIEU

This being contains everything. This book, too. She reminds me why I love literature. Why I love, period. Why I love sentences that go off in thirty-one different directions. As much as those that go just one way. I want to eat pickles. To immolate myself in front of a parliament. It's the simple things that sparkle.

Maybe also you who raises your voice, accelerating the rhythm of the passage for the words that count double. Intertwining, consciously, obsequious, lilliputian, opalescent, iridescent, crepuscular, ingurgitate, serendipity, congeniality, poetry. Latin fever! Sucking the cock of the dictionary! The prize for the best lexicon, on the table at the entrance of the Bibliothèque Nationale, serving shitty bureaucrat wine and a platter full of old cheeses that once belonged to all the great poets of the ages but that taste like sweet fuck all.

MATHIEU

I watch and judge from the swing in the yard. High, low, high, low, bibliographic notes, from the same author or nearly, a bunch of other shit. The poets will send each other chain letters. Send ten glittery cat stickers like these to ten of your friends, making sure to tell them the rules of the chain. Ode, intertexuality, homage. But reactions or criticism, no. There's just one thing left to do. Take out the trash.

And you, little blogger girl, undercover hippie, with your shabby Katimavik logbook, you who take yourself for Jack Kerouac, your penis just the inverted kind. And then, of course, how to forget you, pedant in glasses, for whom love is nothing but the zombification of sexual desire. You with your red ass of adversity. You ate the woman who loves you. A crime of passion, the gun at the back, tickling her vaginal uvula. Now, you regret it. And you, who ate your mother, drove her crazy. And you, your father, you drove him to suicide. Who did you eat to become so beautiful? And how we puffed up the chests of our tales of heart and ass, how we made trilogies of them in order to finally understand that it's the little things that eat the big ones. All to eat us, every one, with our texts and our books. All to reheat the leftovers of every one of us, decade after decade, we became such brilliant microwaves. To everyone, I ask: Is *Pac-Man* a game that plays itself? Is the thousand we can win just a part? Would we not all be wasting our time?

MATHIEU

She's the one who's asking. Are you worth our time?

Instrumental break.
Grumpy violins,
romantic saxophone,
melancholic harp,
devastating harpsichords,
mischievous bell,
eyes you open then close,
metal eyes.
You think the book is over,
you're wrong.
I constantly think life is over.
I'm wrong.
In the end I won't be wrong.
We're all going to die.
I close my eyes.
I'm dead in my sleep.
I open my eyes.
Ding.
I stroll above the heads of my friends.
They're all doing different things.
They all have different things in their hands.
Lives go on.
Raphaëlle shops,
Mathieu corrects the ministerial examinations in French,
Stanislas and Mikka each spoon with their lovers,
my mother cries,
my brother cries,
Anna holds a little poem in her hand.
I close my eyes.
I'm in Banff,

the water is turquoise,
my neck is too.
It's very important that I not put my head underwater.
My technologist says so.
I open my eyes.
Ding.

Oasis of illness
My mother's house
Week 2 – Friday
Diet: Normal
Dinner
Private room
Name: Gendreau, Vickie
Ice cream sandwich
Grilled cheese with meatloaf
Romaine hearts salad
Raspberry vinaigrette
Fresh mint
Salt
Pepper
Diced scorpions
Ketchup dip

Pecan Ensure
Decadron (1)

PAVILION C

VICKIE

Every day since the twenty-second treatment, I think I'm going to die on the X-ray table, that my heart is going to leave my chest, that it'll explode. Panic attacks. I always have to keep my back arched, exaggeratedly arched. My book catches up with me; my illness catches up with me. It usually happens after I've eaten. Palpitations, eyes ringed with black, feeling like a heap of organs with a fuse. It's finished, it's all over. I have to swallow more pills more often to avoid feeling like I'm dying. It's not made up, all this. Nothing here is made up. I'm telling you everything. I go down to the fifth basement, I scan my card so they know I'm here. Vickie Gendreau is wanted in Room L. I go. I wait in one of the two dressing rooms. These rooms are for the people who have to wear a gown for their treatment. I get to stay dressed. The technician girls like what I wear. I always get at least one compliment. That's what girls do when they meet other girls for the first time, give compliments. It's like an automatic mechanism. Dominic usually comes to get me. Today, it's Alex. We're ready, you're ready, let's go into this room and use this machine. Let's try to save you. Alex has long hair in a ponytail and now that I think of it, he looks a bit like a bird. I can give compliments too, I'm a girl. A nervous girl rabbit, complete with frenzied heartbeat. Dominic went on paternity leave. I feel bad, I didn't ask him any questions. Is it a boy or a girl? What's its name? Just congratulations, and it'd been a pleasure. It's been awkward between Dominic and me ever since I said to him as I lay down on the machine: Well, let's go, pin me down on the table, Dominic. They put a white mask with holes in it on my face. The technicians leave. Alex speaks to me over his microphone. The treatment lasts fifteen minutes. Around seven minutes, I start to taste metal in my throat. I have eight more treatments to try to identify this taste.

MAXIME

You didn't come to my funeral or to the celebration of my life. Vickie, I'm dead. I hope you are too. Do you have a number for good MDMA? You can't find it at the grocery store here.

CATHERINE

Why do you have an inflatable doll in your arms, mademoiselle? Where are you going like that? I pass the dépanneur. I end up at Féérique's daycare at night. It's closed. I leave Inflatable Vickie on the pavement and cry. My nose full of snot. It's not pretty. A nightingale perches on my shoulder. I blow my nose with it.

MIKKA

I'm sleeping. I wake up with a start. A boot flew at my head. That'll do it. I get up slowly. There's no coffee left. I get dressed to go buy some. A brown envelope waits for me on the doorstep. There's a red car double-parked. The neighbour is getting a poutine delivered. It's Sunday, it's the day after yesterday, it's her time.

STANISLAS

I go down on Samantha at my place while you do your chemo in your bath. I sent you like ten postcards while I was travelling in the U.S. You told me you'd pinned them up on an ugly IKEA canvas with earrings. You told me that when you were still speaking to me.

VICKIE

Today is July 22, 2012, I'm at the Hôpital Notre-Dame. On May 21, 2012, I was onstage in Rouyn, busy shaking my ass, it was my mother's birthday but turns out it was Pauline's birthday, too, the nurse who takes care of my blood work, and it was also the birthday of my radiology doctor, Dr. Bahary. June 6, 2012, I learned about my tumour, and it was my father's birthday. My father was afraid of having testicular cancer, very afraid, he'd secretly taken a bunch of tests. He showed up at the big results appointment and the doctor came out to call the name of the next patient. Alain Gendreau. Two men got up. There was another Alain Gendreau right there in front of him. This other Alain Gendreau didn't just have the same name as him, but also had an appointment right before his. They had to take out their health cards so that the doctor could match the right results to the right set of balls. Tomorrow is my twenty-fourth treatment. It'll be followed by a massage. It's ten bucks for an hour. By Madame Verdi, who was also born April 14, like me. She remembers it for the Titanic, which sunk on our birthday, but not for Alexandre Jardin. She must really not give a shit about Alexandre Jardin, his last name is Austrian, it's a thousand times more glamorous. Alexander Who? Who cares.

TREATMENT 24.DOC

Machine, I feel like a heap of organs, I'm afraid. Alex is going to have to cut holes in my mask for my nostrils and mouth before tomorrow's treatment. I bought a CD to calm me down. I'm not taking any chances. I went to the Museé d'art contemporain this afternoon. I'd forgotten my hat and the sun in front of the entrance to the museum was relentless. I went into the shade to smoke my cigarettes. The shade made me think of you, machine. I'd like to film you in action. Maybe I should ask my mother to stay with me in the room during the treatment and talk to me. I'll take deep breaths beforehand and during. You exhaust me and you crush my will to live. I feel like a heap of organs with a fuse.

VICKIE

Stanislas, Man I Love Who Doesn't Love Me, edition 2012, I can't talk anymore, about everything, nothing, my treatments. My daily life. Man of my life, but me not the woman of yours, I already spend too much time on Facebook because that's where I meet up with you, it's on Facebook I was going to wait for you. Wait for you to log on so I could talk to you about the new butterfly, the big swallowtail, wait for you to log on to talk to you about my room, wait for you to log on to talk to you about my day, my rose tea, my dark chocolate cookies, everything that livens up my days, in the most infinitesimal detail. My lemon cakes and Isabelle's and my stepfather's, and compare them. Laugh at you, with you. Describe for you in detail the *Zoo* exhibit at the Musée d'art contemporain. The sleeping owl, the crabs that devour themselves, the human skulls set with stones. I feel it, how it's difficult to live without you today. We should have been on the road to Sudbury right now. I would have made cookies for the trip. I would have made sandwiches, the crusts cut off. I would have brought electronic cigarettes, the ones that Francis gave me so I'd smoke less.

RAPHAËLLE

She had the same birthday as her massage therapist, she didn't go to Max's funeral, the series was never recreated. It was always there, wise, waiting for her, waiting for her imminent end. Me and my clothes, my clothes and me, I don't even know where to put myself in the sentence anymore. Do the clothes come first, even today? Today is nobody's birthday. Today, she died.

TREATMENT 25.DOC

The nurse gave me a blue pill before my treatment. I went in, I put my poem down at your machine feet. I gave the Grimes CD to the technician. Skip the first one. He'd made holes in my mask for my nose and mouth. He talked to me the whole time, or maybe it was the girl technician. In any case, I know that I didn't see evil cats that looked like dental scans crowned with fur, unlike yesterday. I saw ink stains. It all seemed soft, soft, soft though. Fuzzy danger. Everything is in the blue pill. It came to save me for the rest of my treatments. I will have to write to it from now on. You understand, beautiful love machine. I have a silly grin and I'm chain-smoking cigarettes. My coffee is hot. The air conditioner is installed. My uncle came by this afternoon. My father is supposed to come by later. He'll leave me some cash. I've gotten pretty poor on welfare. When I was dancing, I could make up to three thousand dollars a week, in Fermont up to five thousand. Eating well was enough of a luxury for me. I like cooking for my friends. They come to visit me in my oasis of illness. I thank them with cookies or chicken thighs in Boursin cheese. I'm not dead yet, I'm not sick of dying but recovering takes a long time. Recovery isn't guaranteed, but we'll try anyway. We'll be the football team and all the cheerleaders at once.

ANNA

I want to make art with her radiation mask. I don't dare talk to her mother or Mathieu about it. It's still too early. I'll have to go to the radiation oncology department and ask. Can I have Vickie's mask, the one you made holes in, two for the nostrils and one for the mouth?

MATHIEU

Anna brought her to the Musée d'art contemporain. Anna brought her to the MAC. Vickie had a Mac. She bequeathed it to me. I put it on my chest. Her mother gave it to me. I emptied it.

TREATMENT 30.DOC

Sweet oval blue pill, you are so beautiful by day and you knock me out so well by night. You bestill my beating heart, my frenzied rabbit heart. Oh sweet gentle pill, with your Viagra-blue complexion, your air of duty-free vacations, you cost me dearly. But oh, you do me good. You do what needs doing, you do it like you should.

VICKIE

It is July 27, 2012. It's Mathieu's real birthday. Every year he picks a fake birthday for himself, usually in September or November. We met on his real birthday. He'd pinned me up against the wall of a shop entrance at the corner of Pins and St-Laur. A short time ago, long ago, when we still wanted each other. Everything is better when it's cerebral rather than corporal. Want more numbers? I'm up to twenty-four and a half pills today. I'm costing the state about three hundred thousand bucks for my treatment. My pivot nurse likes round numbers. I hate every kind of number. I like letters, initials, words (V.G. eats dead animals.) You close your eyes. They bring up the red lights at the back of the stage. "Living Dead Girl" by Rob Zombie starts. A remix from the DJ's computer. If you don't have the original song, you gotta say so, babe. Mathieu is freaking out. He thinks that my fuck-me boots are an adequate choice. He's finally going to see me dance. I don't climb the stairs. I signal to the DJ. He puts on my CD, a little pissed off.

ANNA

Vickie comes into the room, dripping in gold. Dripping in, yeah, that's British slang. Vickie's brain was spattered Pollock-style with freckles and I'm wondering what Picasso drew on his strudels. I watch her spin around her pole in her fuck-me boots and I feel calm. This is how I want to remember her. Naked and golden.

MAMAN

I don't want to watch my daughter take her clothes off. She invited me, she made me come. She wants me to be able to remember everything. Me too. I want to remember her at five years old forever. Still innocent and virginal in that beautiful dress that made her look like a butterfly.

STANISLAS

I don't remember anymore why I stopped wanting to fuck her. All the guys are staring at her, wanting her. She's agile. Miraculous, little feeling.

BROTHER

Go sister, you're the best. Red Car is dancing around the little pole in my hand. I keep thinking how Red Car could be anywhere, that it could be anyone here. You got me in. They know I'm too young, but they don't seem to care. First dance of the afternoon shift. I wanna remember you just like this. Legs entwined at the zenith of the pole. My sister is more flexible than your sister.

VICKIE

The fast one's done, go for the slow. "The Hardest Button to Button," the Golden Filter remix, starts. I climb back onto the stage in my multicoloured dress.

DJ

And now, please welcome to the stage the Very Sensual Lily! Followed back to back by the Excellent Kimora! Make some noise for a lesbian show! These girls eat each other out for real!

VICKIE

My dress looks like a harp, I play a riff, twist my nipple for the distortion. My pedals come up to my mid-thigh, more grip on the pole, I hang my head upside down. On the beat, always on the beat, I quickly descend to the floor. My heels resonate on the stainless steel, the echo strikes my chest, I slip off my G-string. On the beat, zig-zagging it down low, on the beat. Always on the beat.

I close my eyes, I open my eyes.
One thing a day, one step, one red agenda.
I'm going somewhere.
I'm talking to someone.
I close my eyes, I open my eyes.
I look out the window.
I close an eye, type with one hand.
The wisp of smoke.
My skin has many colours.
I sat out in the sun for more than twenty but less than
    thirty minutes, to look a little less sick.
I think about the sound recordist for *Archives de l'âme*,
    the documentary about the Nuit de la poésie in 1970.
I thought about him a few times this week.
I like imagining his voice.
His life spent capturing the voices of others on defective
    microphones.
Everything, absolutely everything, and nothing.
I'll remember everything, it's required.
Especially the silences.
I keep my eyes closed a long time.

To Anna, I bequeath:
five little poems,
this leopard-print scarf
and one hundred fennec foxes.

ANNA

The nurse had told her mother that one should never stop believing in miracles. That's fucking heavy. You don't want people talking about miracles when they're discussing your recovery. Take some cookies with you Anna, Vickie was always saying to me. She'd made me cookies that had pudding mix in them, so they'd stay soft. She made them during her break from the hospital. She bought little lime-green boxes to package them. The USB key is lime-green too, the envelope is brown, the book is purple.

NINJA.DOC

the stuffed tortoise
on my desk
watches me watch
the blank document
there's at least that to write

I don't ask for much. I get along with myself very well, I'm independent. But recently: the apparition of a boy. My bed suddenly seems so small. I wonder if, once the soles of his shoes wear out, his feet smell like two girls tied for first in a wet T-shirt contest. I met this boy two weeks ago. It's doomed, I'm moving to Ottawa. I offer him a cookie anyway. Just one bite. It's enough. Believe me. These are impossible to resist. But try. Just one. There are books you should avoid studying too closely. There are cookies it would be best to avoid eating. Return, purchase, list, leave without finishing it. A, b, c, d, e, f, g, h, i want, j, k, l, make love to me, n, oops just kidding, p, q, r, s, t, u, v, w, x, you stimulate my ventral tegmental area, z. I love you, me neither. Gulp.

WHITE TRASH.DOC

the albino lion on top
of the food chain
it would be thus
if the entire jungle
swam in bleach
the sun lightens my hair
i'm in the race
in the bleachers everyone's cheering
i pick my teeth with the javelin
safe
on the bench
i could make myself brooches with the railway ties

safe
on the bench
but i'll say something smart
again

ANNA

The squirrel is making himself a nest in the crook of the
tree outside my window. The squirrel is a friend of mine.
He has a tiny brain. He often forgets us. Like right now,
he's perched on the neighbour's ladder, on the look-out,
staring at me. "I, squirrel, I, surveillance camera." The
jerky movements of his head set up different shots on
the camera's monitor. A stop-motion of my tender gaze
in his direction. I've become buddy-buddy with rodents
since I started reading poetry.

CHANTILLY.DOC

alight
bright
i'd like a light switch in my leggings
head of the bedside table
a big drawer
a smaller one
of lubricant
i'd like a make-up holiday
the same flowered shirt
but fewer accessories
filthy boxers
dirty without even having been worn

147

The last time I moved, all my possessions fit into a case of beer. Today, it's in a pack of cigarettes. I don't even smoke, I just travel light. I'll put away as many things as possible in the little green boxes she used to package the cookies she gave me. My jewellery, to start. The earrings I bought myself in the Namur metro, my necklaces, my rings, and I'm out of space already. I'll put all the little poems she left to me in the mead bottle once it's empty. I'll write "Molotov Cocktail" on the label.

BOMBAY SAPPHIC.DOC

the pool has parted its lips
taken off its jacket
put away the winter clothes
a few blocks of ice
giant gin and tonic
the day
opens wide
a big-bellied sale
a milk belly
summer is a beautiful girl who thinks she's ugly

ANNA

We're all together in Parc Laurier for the celebration of her life. Everyone's drinking. Mathieu has microbrewery beer, I have the bottle of mead I opened yesterday. Stanislas and Mikka aren't here. Catherine is drinking wine with Samson. They bought an inflatable doll at a sex shop. She's in the red bag on the table. I like that people brought drinks. I don't know everyone. They arrived too late. Turn on the lights. Party's over. Whatever. They're here, anyway. It looks good on a CV, to have shown up at the celebration of life of a girl they knew, and especially to have brought wine glasses. It's a good conversation piece. Anyway. I have a lot of respect for the people drinking their booze in little glasses with a few ice cubes and maybe another ingredient to poeticize the experience. There are so many poets here. All the better. All the squirrels here want to be my friend. The mead attracts them. Maybe it's also the melancholy… I don't drink to forget but to cope. This bottle to find the courage to read this last poem. I open my damp eyes.

WAVES.DOC

what if we went down south
right now
to look at the waves
without saying a word
for five years time

Translator's Note

I was immediately captivated by Vickie Gendreau's voice on my first reading of *Testament*, her voice and the fierce, urgent intimacy of her text and its gorgeous audacity. I knew right away that I wanted to translate it and I also knew what a challenge it would be. This most imperative of autofictions, written in the face of fatal illness, demands a sort of reverence from the translator who would "rewrite" it. And yet the translator has to feel free to make the decisions that will best write the text into a new language.

Testament pulls the reader in close and then sometimes doesn't let her in on the joke. We are invited into these texts that serve as last testaments, her final addresses to the people in her life, and find ourselves occasionally eavesdropping on snippets of conversation for which we have little context, smiling at inside jokes we don't really understand. Gendreau moves between the present and the near-future, between poetry and prose, between French and English. Her textured, hybrid language – a French that mixes and mingles with English – was a particular challenge in translation. I feared erasing her use of English and wanted to preserve this beautiful, fluid mingling of languages. My first instinct was to mark her English, to "translate" it by italicizing it. But this strategy, it turned out, rather missed the point. Italics are often used to signal the foreign, the so-called "exotic," the interjection of another language; in some English translations of Québécois literature, italics have been used to mark the authors' (often pointed or politicized) uses of English in the original French text. But Gendreau's English is one both of a new generation of Québécois writers and artists, and at the same time all her own. It was one of her languages, one she felt at home in. Marking her use of English words and phrases, which are a seamless part of the novel, its rhythms and its poetry, was clumsy, and it belied her relation to the language, making foreign what was not.

And so, in the end, I have not marked the words or phrases that were written in English in the original. The occasional French words or phrases that remain in the translation also appear in straight text, in the hopes of at least gesturing toward the hybrid, idiosyncratic language of Gendreau's original text. And yet, French in an English text still *means* differently than English in a French text; one cannot replace the other in any kind of one-to-one ratio, and so my efforts to compensate for the disappearance of Gendreau's English into an English-language translation must remain but a gesture.

I did not get the chance to meet Vickie Gendreau, or discuss her text and its translation with her. I have, however, had much help from many people along the way. I am grateful for Sherry Simon's support of this project from the beginning – her careful reading of drafts both early and late and her guidance throughout the process were invaluable. Éric de Larochellière of Le Quartanier and Mathieu Arsenault gave helpful notes and important insights into the text, particularly on the question of "translating" the novel's original English. Einar Jullum Leiknes has been a patient reader of this translation and a source of unwavering support and surprising and inspired ideas. Finally, a most special thanks to Jay and Hazel at BookThug for sharing my enthusiasm for this *Testament* and making a home for it in English.

— Aimee Wall

Colophon

Distributed in Canada by the Literary Press Group:
www.lpg.ca

Distributed in the United States by Small Press Distribution:
www.spdbooks.org

Shop online at www.bookthug.ca

Designed by Malcolm Sutton
Copy edited by Ruth Zuchter

BOOK
PRODUCTION
WAR ECONOMY
STANDARD